STOLEN
BY HER BEAR
BLACK RIDGE BEARS BOOK 1

FELICITY HEATON

THE BLACK RIDGE BEARS SERIES

Book 1: Stolen by her Bear

Book 2: Rescued by her Bear

Book 3: Saved by her Bear

Book 4: Unleashed by her Bear

Book 5: Awakened by her Bear

The Black Ridge Bears series is part of the Eternal Mates World, which includes the Eternal Mates series, Cougar Creek Mates series, and the London Vampires series.

Discover more available paranormal romance books at:
http://www.felicityheaton.com

Or sign up to my mailing list to receive a FREE vampire romance ebook, learn about new titles, be eligible for special subscriber-only giveaways, and read exclusive content including short stories:
http://ml.felicityheaton.com/mailinglist

CHAPTER 1

The noise came again, dragging him up from a deep sleep. Saint's ears twitched and he tried to shut out the sound, burrowed deeper beneath the pile of furs and shuffled the pillow over his head. He hooked his arm over it, pressing it to his ear.

His mind emptied, the waiting arms of sleep that hadn't quite released him pulling him back into the darkness.

He sank into it.

Growled as the distant laughter pulled him back up.

They just weren't going to shut up.

He needed them to shut up!

His thoughts blurred, heavy intangible things that bled together with his bear instincts, had his actions sluggish as he tossed the furs off him and tried to sit up. His whole body felt too heavy, his limbs like lead as he wearily blinked, as he fought to lift his right hand and rub the sleep from his eyes. Another growl rumbled from his chest as he heard the noise again, part of him straining to catch it whenever it happened now, so tuned into it that he could only focus on it, making sleep impossible.

Irritation flared hotter in his veins as he glared at the small window on the gable end of his cabin to his right.

A blackout blind obscured his view of the world, but he would bet his left nut that it wasn't spring yet.

Saint yawned as he pushed onto his feet, grumbled a curse as he had to grip the pitched ceiling to stop himself from falling on his ass when his knees weakened, unused to bearing his weight. He must have been asleep for a while at least, possibly a few weeks. Not nearly enough of them to get him through the winter.

His bear side growled and swayed, filled him with a black need to roar and lash out at the world.

He just wanted to sleep.

Saint stumbled to the wooden spiral staircase that led down from his loft bedroom, took each step carefully as control of his body slowly came back to him and he began to shake off the effects of his winter sleep. His stomach growled as loudly as his bear instincts, and he rubbed it through his cream long johns, his mouth watering as his mind turned to steak. It would have to wait.

First thing he needed to do was find out who the hell was making that ruckus.

Maybe if he knew who it was, knew it wasn't a threat to him and his kin, he could finally shift his focus back to sleeping.

He gripped the newel post at the bottom of the staircase and rubbed his dark eyes again, unleashed another yawn that was so big he was in danger of snapping his jaw off.

Saint grimaced as he placed one foot on the wooden floor of his cabin and quickly snatched it back to set it on the last step of the staircase. He glared at the freezing cold boards and then his gaze leaped to his slippers. A curse pealed from his lips. He had left them near the worn dark brown couch that had its back to him, faced the log burner and the wooden wall opposite him. He had always been the kind of bear to hibernate through the winter, sleeping the short frigid days away, dreaming of spring. He should have spotted the signs that the winter sleep was upon him, should have known it would be months before he woke again, and that the cabin would be freezing by the time spring roused him.

Saint switched the order of things.

First port of call was getting the fire going.

He pulled a face at the frigid floor and then went for it, swore when he tried to move too fast for his recovering body and slammed into the back of the couch, ending up bent over it. He huffed and grabbed his slippers, was swift to tug them on.

Saint scratched his backside as he yawned and trudged to the black log burner. He sank in front of it and cleaned it out, set up a new fire and lit it. Stared at it as the kindling caught and flames began to dance around the split logs. Warmth curled around him, tugged another yawn from him as a desire to go back to bed and back to sleep filled him.

Gods, he just wanted to sleep.

He dragged a hand down his face, over a month's growth of beard. He couldn't sleep though. Not until he knew the source of the noise.

He had a duty to ensure his pride were safe. Only the twins, Knox and Lowe, were overwintering with him at Black Ridge, their territory deep in a valley in British Columbia, Canada, but that didn't change his duty as their alpha. He had to make sure it wasn't hunters or humans out there in the valley.

Although, he had the feeling he knew who was making that ruckus.

He growled low, forced himself to leave the fire and grabbed his thick black and green checked fleece from the back of the couch. He tugged the padded shirt on, buttoned it as he moved to the door to the right of his small kitchen. Another growl rolled from him as he shifted the blackout blind on the door aside and flinched, the brightness of the sun bouncing off the thick layer of snow outside almost blinding him.

He was going to need more than a fleece and jeans to check out what was happening.

He huffed as he pivoted on his heel, as he crossed the room to the far end and the tall cupboards that filled the space on the right of it, beneath one corner of his loft bedroom. He yanked the wooden doors open and grabbed a heavy winter jacket and thick waterproof trousers, kicked off his slippers and pulled the clothing on. He bent and rifled around in the bottom of the cupboard, snarled when he didn't find what he was looking for.

Saint slammed the doors, his mood degenerating rapidly as the thought of all the snow that waited outside, blanketing his territory, only strengthened his desire to sleep, until it fogged his mind and had his limbs feeling heavy again.

He tried to shake off his bear instincts as he opened the next cupboard and found what he was looking for in the bottom of it. He grabbed his heavy fleece-lined winter boots and pulled the socks he had bundled into balls out of them as he stomped to the couch. A couch that felt too inviting as he sank onto it to tug the thermal socks onto his feet, made him want to roll onto his side and just sleep.

The noise came again.

Fuck sleep.

He was going to kill whoever was out there disturbing his peace.

He yanked the socks on, followed them with the boots, and shoved to his feet, stormed to the door and pulled it open. A foot of snow cascaded into his home, covering his boots, and he looked down at it.

Roared as he kicked at it, frustration getting the better of him. "Get the fuck out of my home."

"Someone woke up on the wrong side of the bed." The deep male voice that drawled that at him came from his right, and had his focus shifting there.

His eyes watered as the bright snow assaulted them and he blinked to clear his vision as he stepped out onto the deck of his cabin and tugged the door closed behind him. He looked to his right, but the overhanging pitched roof that provided some protection for the front of his cabin obscured his view, forcing him to move to the wooden railing that enclosed the deck.

Saint leaned against the capping rail and looked across the deep blanket of snow to the twin cabins that were closer to the trees on that side of the clearing that formed the heart of Black Ridge. Beyond those cabins, the forest rose up the side of the towering mountains that sheltered his territory, the dark evergreen canopy capped with white as far as the eye could see.

He grunted at all the snow.

Knox stood by the door of the cabin on the left of the two, looking just as grumpy as Saint felt, wrapped in a thick checked robe and sneering at the snow.

The sandy-haired bear wasn't the only one awake either.

Saint glanced at the cabin to the right of Knox's, at the more ash-blond male who was shovelling snow off his deck, and who, unlike his twin, was already wearing sensible winter protective gear.

Had Saint woken the brothers from their winter sleep, or had it been that damned noise?

He cocked his head as he listened for it, starting to think maybe he had imagined it.

But then another round of raucous laughter and cheering echoed through the trees.

Trees that stretched from the foothills of the mountains on his right to the river hidden somewhere beneath the snow to Saint's left, separating Black Ridge from Cougar Creek.

Saint growled again as he twisted to face that way, his fangs dropping this time and a need to shift surging through him. Damned cougars. It had to be them. No human was insane enough to venture up the valley in the dead of winter, when the snow drifted to over six feet deep in places.

But it wasn't like the cougar shifters to be noisy in winter.

They were usually silent once the snow began to creep further down the mountains and began to fall in the basin of the valley, the last of the visitors bidding goodbye to Cougar Creek for the year, leaving their alpha, Rath, alone there throughout the long winter months.

Saint poked his head out from beneath the protruding roof of his cabin and glared at the sun where it skimmed just above the mountains to his left, on the rise. Normally, he enjoyed seeing the sun shining against the vivid blue sky, liked gazing at the jagged mountains and the dense forests that covered the land on that side of the creek.

Loved lazing by that creek, watching the fish.

Couldn't do that now, with it buried under several feet of snow and ice.

He turned his frown on the snow that reached almost as high as the deck, had to be at least three feet deep where it had accumulated against the underside of his raised cabin. His gaze tracked across the undulating snow that stretched between him and the thick forest of lodgepole pines and spruces.

This was going to be one shitty walk.

Putting it off wasn't going to make it any nicer though, or make his mood any better.

He wasn't the only grouchy bear on the property either. He glanced to his right at Knox and Lowe, could see by their faces they were as pissed as he was by the disturbance. Having the three of them tired and grumpy would only make all of them worse in the long run, would bring out the bear in them and cause them to bicker and fight, destroying the peace they normally enjoyed. So as much as he despised the thought of dropping down into three feet of snow, he was going to have to do it.

Gods, he was glad Rune and Maverick had gone to Vancouver for winter as they always did, the two of them travelling to a bolthole they shared there. Neither of them was the sort of bear to sleep the months away, preferred to be awake through winter, but like him, they didn't like snow. Saint had once made the mistake of convincing them to stay at Black Ridge for winter, had denied the urge to sleep so he could stay awake with them.

It hadn't gone well.

They had made it to December before Rune and Maverick had gotten into a brawl so bad he had feared they would kill each other, and then all three of them had holed up in their individual cabins until the snowmelt. It had been the longest damned winter of Saint's life. He hadn't been able to sleep, had stayed awake to make sure Rune and Maverick made it to spring.

He scrubbed a hand over his beard, hoping like hell things didn't end up that bad this time. If they couldn't get back to sleep, ended up having to stay awake, then he wasn't sure he would be able to keep his cool and smooth the edge of his own mood to maintain order within their makeshift pride.

As it was, he was itching for a fight.

If Knox or Lowe tried to start anything, just looked at him the wrong way, he was liable to blow his top.

Knox kicked the snow off his deck, grumbling, "I'm tempted to go deal with whoever is making all that noise."

"Rein it in, or I'll be tempted to deal with you," Lowe muttered as he finished pushing the last of the snow off his own deck, piling it up around the thick wooden pylons that raised the cabin off the ground.

It wasn't like the usually laid-back Lowe to be grumpy. Normally, the ash-blond bear took things as they came, rolling with whatever life threw at him without worrying too much. Saint blamed Knox's mood. It was his brother's agitation that had Lowe on edge too.

Lowe always got like this whenever Knox was fired up, felt a need to weigh in and have his twin's back.

"I'll go see what the deal is." Saint turned away from them and murmured under his breath, "Just got to get through this crap first."

He huffed and took the first step down from his deck, forced himself to keep going when the next one was hidden by snow. His pride needed him to do something, and he would do it. He would make the cougars shut up so he and his kin could get back to sleep, and when he woke, all the snow would be gone.

He held on to that fantasy, filling his mind with images of green grass and warm sunshine as he trudged down the steps. It shattered as he fumbled for the final step and slipped, had to grab the railing behind him and brace himself to avoid falling on his backside.

Saint growled as he pushed away from the steps and waded through the deep snow, heading for the forest that would lead him to Cougar Creek. He glared at the field of white as it sparkled, the weak sunlight reflecting off it enough to almost blind him. As it was, it made his eyes water again, and that moisture felt as if it was turning to ice in his eyes.

There was nothing magical about winter.

He huffed and snarled as he pushed forwards, ploughing a path through the snow. At least he wouldn't get as cold and damp on the way back, after he was done murdering whoever had woken him and his kin.

If he somehow managed to rein in the urge to spill blood, maybe the fresh air and struggling through the snow would tire him out enough that he could sleep when he got back to his cabin.

He finally reached the dense forest, where most of the snow clung to the branches of the pines and firs, keeping the amount on the ground down to less than a foot. He picked his way through the fresh snow, careful not to snag his boot on a root or rock because falling flat on his face in the snow would probably be the match that lit the fuse of his temper.

Saint breathed a little easier as he reached an animal track, a path through the forest that had been kept clear of snow by the constant back and forth of the local ungulates. His muscles began to relax, the tension that had stiffened them during the walk through the icy snow fading as he picked up pace.

When he neared the invisible boundary between Cougar Creek and Black Ridge, he slowed and fell silent, his breathing levelling out as he moved with stealth into the trees, veering off the track. His ears twitched as he listened, the only sound that of distant birdsong and animals moving through the trees. No laughter. No voices.

His breath fogged in the air as he slipped from tree to tree, peering ahead of him through the trunks and low branches and the scrub, seeking a sign of life as he drew closer to Cougar Creek. His palms began to sweat as his heart drummed a faster, harder rhythm against his ribs, as he honed his senses and searched for danger, in case it was hunters who had come to the cougar territory and they were the ones laughing.

Overjoyed by capturing or killing a shifter.

He spat on the ground, cursing the hunters. They had taken too many from his kin.

Had taken too much from him.

He had barely matured, had only just passed a century old when the mortal hunter organisation Archangel had executed a raid on a nearby underground fae town. His parents had been there, had tried to escape and hadn't made it out alive.

Last year, a helicopter had circled over Black Ridge, heading back to Cougar Creek, and Saint had heard the distant gunfire. Part of him had wanted to go and check it out, to see if Rath needed help.

The rest, the alpha in him, had made him stay at Black Ridge in case there were more hunters in the forests and his pride needed him.

He tipped his head up and dragged in a slow, deep breath as he pushed those memories aside, focusing on the present in case it was hunters. He couldn't let himself get swept up in the past, had to stay alert and aware of his surroundings and any danger that might be lying in wait for him.

Saint scented the air, trying to catch something that would tell him what to expect ahead of him.

He froze, locked up tight as he caught a scent, as warmth spread through him in response, roused a hunger in him that was powerful and commanding.

He dragged in another breath, aching for another delectable hit of that scent. And it was *delectable*, like sweet berries, and utterly feminine.

Which was enough to set him on edge.

Females didn't stay at Cougar Creek in winter.

Saint veered off course again, unable to stop himself from tracking the scent through the forest, curiosity gripping him and filling him with a need to find the owner of it. His mouth watered, the hunger clenching his gut growing fiercer as the scent grew stronger. Ahead of him, the bushes and trees gave way to man-made clearings, openings in the forest where small cabins had been constructed.

He huffed.

Cougar Creek.

He stealthily inspected the two cabins he could see, keeping his distance from them. Snow had fallen through the canopy of the forest and was thick on their roofs, and it was pristine on the decks, untouched. No one was staying in them.

Saint banked left, heading down towards the river, to a cabin he knew was there. The raised L-shaped wooden lodge sat at the head of a fifty-foot clearing in the forest, one that stretched down to the creek.

He remained in the shadows of the trees as he moved towards that river, giving the place a wide berth. He eyed the deck and the steps and the ground just beyond them. Someone had cleared the snow away. The place belonged to one of the three brothers of Rath, the alpha of the pride, and it was usually empty over winter.

Looked as if the male was staying this time.

Was he responsible for the ruckus that had woken Saint and his kin?

He sharpened his instincts again and frowned as he sensed more than just Rath and one brother at the Creek. He pinpointed at least five other people, most of them close to the main clearing. One of them was bound to be the female Rath had mated with last year, one Saint had seen for himself a few times.

He thought her name was Ivy, was sure he had heard the alpha cougar call her that a few times when she had been photographing bears near the river. The female was human, and not the only one at the Creek either.

The bastard Storm had a human female of his own. Saint had caught her in the woods last year when she had been running from the male and had scared her witless. He regretted what had happened now, but he had been in a foul mood, his bear at the fore. Their run-in had happened only a week after the Archangel helicopter had come and the need to protect his kin had been strong, fierce enough that he had viewed her as a threat.

Saint had figured Gabi for a huntress, still thought she was a member of Archangel and one day Storm was going to wake up to find a blade in his heart.

He backtracked up to the two empty cabins and headed past them into another area of dense scrub that provided cover as he moved towards the heart of Cougar Creek.

His ears twitched.

Voices.

He eased lower and peered through the bushes and trees towards the clearing. Stilled as he spotted two males and a female in an area that had been cleared of snow near the top of the long sloping strip of green that formed the centre of the cougar's territory. The felines had been busy. It looked as if they had cleared snow in a patch roughly sixty feet in all directions from the front of Rath's cabin. That cabin sat nestled among the pines and spruces, its back to the forest that covered the base of the mountain, facing the clearing and the creek at the bottom of it.

What were they up to?

Rath straightened and planted the tip of his snow shovel against the ground, leaned on the handle of it as he pushed his thick black hat up and wiped his brow. He pulled his dark green scarf down and undid the top fastening of his black winter jacket.

"We taking a break now?" the male with him growled, a hint of warmth and teasing in his tone as he set down his own shovel and tugged at the blue scarf wrapped around his throat. Like Rath, he wore a black protective coat and matching hat, and irritatingly kept his back to Saint so he couldn't make out which brother he was. "Only been at it an hour. Still a lot more snow to clear."

Rath huffed and scrubbed a hand down his face, over a thick dark beard. "Remind me again why we're doing this."

The big male chuckled, the warmth in his voice lingering. "Love, apparently. Not sure why I got pulled into shovelling duties though. Storm should be here, clearing the way for this ceremony. Where is he anyway?"

This time, Rath was the one who chuckled, his grey eyes brightening with it. "Where do you think?"

The male shook his head. "I have half a mind to go bang down his door, but I don't want to get an eyeful. Flint could at least have offered to help, but he's about as useful as Storm."

Flint and Storm weren't present then, which meant the big male with Rath was Cobalt. Cobalt was a mad bastard. Saint had never seen a cougar fight like he did, as if he had nothing left to live for.

Rath and Cobalt were as big as each other, packed with muscle and good fighters, but if it came to a one-on-one fight, Saint could take them. Provided they didn't resort to low blows like their brother Flint.

He shuddered at the memory, his balls aching. It had taken him weeks to heal them after the male had run his claws over them during a brawl. He still hadn't forgiven the cougar, wanted a piece of him, and Storm, for the scars they had given him. A low growl curled up his throat, his blood running hot despite the cold, and he wanted to unleash it but bit it back instead. As much as he wanted a fight, he wanted to sleep more.

Besides, he couldn't let his foul mood get him into a brawl right now when his body was still recovering from a month-long sleep. He would probably lose and that would only make his mood worse.

Saint drew down a steadying breath and stilled as the delicious scent of berries hit him again. It was weaker now, but still warmed him, roused a hunger to hunt the owner of that scent and see her for himself.

The door of the cabin behind Rath opened and a female came out, wrapped so heavily in winter clothing that he couldn't make out much of her face between her colourful striped scarf and woollen hat, or her figure through the thick cream coat and brown ski pants.

He knew her scent though.

Ivy.

In fact, he knew most of the scents of the females belonging to the brothers. He had put Gabi's scent to memory when he had captured her, and he had done the same with Yasmin's when Flint had come to Black Ridge looking for a fight in order to impress her.

Maybe he had imagined the sweet scent in the woods.

Berries were his vice after all.

He loved them and found them impossible to resist.

"Come warm up for a few minutes." She looked at her mate and then at Cobalt.

Both males nodded and let their shovels fall into the thin layer of snow, and Rath waited for Cobalt to reach him before they both started towards the cabin.

"Does Ember want to drop in for a warming drink too?" Ivy said with a look at Cobalt.

Ember. Saint wasn't familiar with that female.

"She went for a walk." Cobalt tugged his black hat off, revealing mussed blond hair. "But she'll be back in time for the practice run."

Rath glanced at his brother. "Did your certificate come through?"

"Yup. I'm officially ordained." Cobalt flashed a grin at him and chuckled. "That's not something I ever thought I would be. Not many cougars out there needing this sort of thing."

Saint watched them go inside, debated going to the cabin and speaking to Rath, but fatigue was rolling up on him, his eyelids feeling heavy again as the fresh air lost its effect on him and his bear instincts growled at him to go back to sleep. He knew what the noise was now. It wasn't humans or danger, just a bunch of irritating cougars celebrating something. That should be enough to calm the instinct to protect himself and his pride, and allow all of them to get back to sleep.

He rose to his feet and turned away from the cabin, picked his way to the animal track and followed it back towards the Ridge. Maybe he would fix himself some food before he hit the sack again, something to take the edge off his hunger and tide him over while he slept. He was clearly hungry.

Because he was fantasising about sweet juicy summer berries again.

Could smell them stronger now.

He frowned and slowed his pace, lifted his head and drew down a breath. The scent *was* stronger. His mouth watered, heat suffusing him, and he pivoted on his heel, was tracking the smell of berries before he realised what he was doing.

Saint dropped to his haunches when he spotted a lone figure ahead of him, near the frozen river.

A female.

He dragged down a breath, every inch of him locking up tight as he caught her scent.

Sweet berries and a hint of vanilla.

He scented something else on her too. She was cougar. Was she Ember? Did she belong to Cobalt?

Saint told himself to go, but found himself easing lower instead to observe her. Silent. A predator.

She tilted her head up as she turned, raised her gloved hand to cover her eyes as she peered at the canopy. Birds sang there but he paid them no heed, was too arrested by the sight of her.

Raven hair spilled from beneath her dark purple woollen hat, cascading over a form-fitting weatherproof coat in the same colour, and grey eyes with a strong hint of emerald sparkled as rosy lips curled into the semblance of a smile.

His heart started at a hard pace, drumming against his ribs as his blood heated.

She was beautiful.

A need to stand and go to her pounded inside him and he struggled to deny it, to remain where he was and merely observe her, studying everything about her. Like the fact she had to stand at least a foot shorter than his six-seven, and looked as if she weighed nothing more than a feather. There was a delicate sense of beauty about her, with her porcelain skin and the hint of pink on her cheeks, and he lost himself in watching her, the world around him fading away.

Until there was only her.

Her slender shoulders suddenly stiffened, her smile disappearing as she tensed and went still.

She had sensed him.

Saint lingered, wondering what she would do. Run away or stay?

Seconds seemed to stretch into an eternity as he waited, as her grey-green eyes slowly took in the forest.

Strange disappointment flooded him when she suddenly turned on her heel and walked in the direction of Cougar Creek, her pace brisk, boots chewing up the frozen ground beneath the pines.

Saint stared after her.

Driven to follow.

CHAPTER 2

Holly had come to Ember's lodge for some company, but it didn't look as if she was going to get it as her best friend slid an appreciative look down the back of her mate, Cobalt, where he worked in the kitchen to fix them both a cup of hot chocolate before he went out to work on clearing the snow. When Ember had convinced her to come to Cougar Creek for the winter wedding as her plus one, Holly had been excited and eager to escape her family over the holidays.

A time when her three older brothers, and even her parents, loved to tease her about another year passing without her finding a male she was interested in.

It had only been twelve years since she had matured at a century old, but her family were eager for her to find a male. Her transition into cougar shifter adulthood should have awakened her libido.

It had done nothing.

She still didn't feel any spark whenever she was around men, whether they were cougar, human or other. Some of the ones she had tried dating were handsome enough, and she had expected to feel something when she had been with them, a tiny spark of passion.

But she had felt nothing.

Not even an inkling of desire.

She was beginning to think she was dysfunctional.

Escaping to Cougar Creek to avoid another holiday season filled with jibes and interrogations, daily inquests into her dead-on-arrival private life, had sounded like a great idea when Ember had suggested it.

Only Holly had forgotten to account for the fact she was sharing the creek with mated couples only, and it was driving her a little mad to say the least. Ember and Cobalt did their best to include her in things, but she felt like a fifth wheel, as if she was getting in the way of the newly-mated couple all the time. Rath and Ivy were inclusive too, and Storm and Gabi, the other couple who had come here to participate in the joint wedding ceremony and celebration, tried their best but they were normally too busy giving each other moon eyes to notice her.

She couldn't remember the last time she had seen Flint and Yasmin. She felt twenty-percent sure she had seen them arrive, but since then, the two of them had been holed up in Flint's cabin deep in the woods across the clearing from Ember's.

Holly was glad for one thing though—Cobalt had insisted on her staying in his own smaller cabin in the woods while he and Ember shared this one. Ember had done her best to convince her to stay here too, but Cobalt had given her the hard sell. His cabin had a modern kitchen and furniture, a running shower and a hot tub fed by a natural spring.

Ember had been worried Holly would feel isolated there, but she had always loved Cobalt's cabin.

It was peaceful, the small parcel of land that stretched down to the creek always quiet, and it felt like a hundred miles away from the bustle at the main area of the pride's territory and a million miles away from the craziness she would have been in the middle of had she stayed home with her family.

Ember paused at her work sorting through a tangle of white string lights and glanced at Holly, her grey-blue eyes warm as the firelight glinted off them. "So, what was this book about?"

Holly sank back into the wine-red couch in front of the large stone fireplace and pulled her feet up onto the seat of it. "Some cowboy riding in to save the day and whisking the heroine away to live on his ranch in Montana."

"Sounds exactly like the last one you read." Cobalt shook his head and she was tempted to pick up one of the unlit candles from the side table and hurl it at his back.

From the moment he had realised she was spending her time in his cabin reading romance novels, he had been rolling his eyes and shaking his head whenever Ember asked her about them.

"You need to get yourself a real man." The big blond male twisted away from the kitchen and crossed the floor to them, set a mug down in front of her on the wooden coffee table and then one in front of Ember.

Holly clammed up.

Apparently, she couldn't escape people probing into her private life at this time of year, no matter where she went. She knew he meant well, but it still rankled her.

"Cobalt," Ember admonished, but there wasn't any real anger in her tone.

He shrugged, rolling his broad shoulders beneath a thick, black cable-knit jumper. "I'm just saying."

"I don't need a male to make me happy." Holly couldn't hold back those words, ones she had said so many times to her family over the last few years. When Ember gave her a look, guilt churned in her gut and she was quick to add, "I mean, it's lovely that you found your mate, but I'm happy as I am, for now."

That was the first time she had admitted to herself that part of her hoped this whole situation was just that—for now. Not forever. Gods, she didn't want to end up some spinster cougar rattling around lecturing the young like a few of the teachers who had been at her and Ember's school. She would sooner die than spend her entire life without experiencing any sort of spark.

Without knowing the feel of a male's hands on her, or his breath on her neck.

Or his lips claiming hers.

She grabbed her drink and sipped it, hid in it as Cobalt slid down from the arm of the couch to nestle against Ember. Heat filled his grey eyes, bringing out the gold as he gazed at his mate.

Jealousy writhed inside Holly and not for the first time since Cobalt and Ember had picked her up to bring her to the Creek. She tried not to look at them, tried to shut them out as they smiled at each other, as they toyed with each other's hands and spoke in low voices.

They looked so good together, and they were clearly deeply in love, and here she was, unable to feel a damned thing.

Cobalt's grey-gold eyes warmed further. There was so much love in that look.

She felt sure no one would ever look at her that way.

Holly set her drink down and stood, and Ember looked up at her, surprise in her grey-blue eyes that turned to guilt as she eased away from her mate and tucked her fall of wavy black hair behind her ear.

"I'm sorry," Ember whispered.

Holly waved her away. "Don't be. I think I hear another book calling."

Before her friend could say anything else, she grabbed her purple jacket from the rack near the door by the kitchen and pulled her matching hat on, covering her own dark hair. She shoved her feet into her tall waterproof boots and slipped her arms into her coat.

"Thanks for the drink." She regretted turning to say that when she found Cobalt kissing Ember, his right hand framing her face.

Holly hurried out of the door, needing the air.

She stepped off the raised wooden deck of the L-shaped cabin, the snow crunching beneath her boots as she banked right, heading past the huge lodgepole pine that stood in the bend of the cabin. She kept her steps light as she walked, nimbly crossing a patch of slippery compacted snow, and glanced up the sloping clearing towards the far end of it, where the forest was untouched, covered the base of the mountain that watched over the Creek.

Smoke curled lazily from the chimney of the cabin tucked beneath the trees at the top of the clearing, a small lodge with a deck below the pitched roof. Someone moved around inside it, stepping in front of the picture window to the right of the door, and in the triangular window that filled the space right beneath the roof, warm light flickered.

Rath opened the door and stepped out, turned back towards the inside of the cabin and said something she didn't hear. He pulled a black hat on and grabbed the two snow shovels on the deck, and stepped down onto the patch of grass he and his brothers had already worked to clear.

It looked as if Cobalt was about to get another disturbance.

She slipped into the woods to her right, slowly relaxing as she breathed deep of the crisp air, as her gaze darted over everything. Cougar Creek was beautiful in the snow. Peaceful. Sunlight filtered through the trees, caught on the snow that had made it through the branches of the evergreens and made it sparkle like diamonds.

Holly listened to the world, enjoying the quiet of winter, the bite to the air and the chill on her skin. Birds sang in the distance, and more than one creature moved through the trees ahead of her and above her.

She reached Cobalt's cabin but rather than taking the steps up onto the raised deck of the smaller L-shaped wooden lodge that faced a patch of open land and the river, she picked another path, heading down towards that creek.

She listened for it, smiled when she heard it trickling beneath the ice and layers of snow.

Holly stopped close to the concealed bank of it, drew down a deep breath and sighed it out as she gazed at the snow-draped forest that covered the other side of the river, followed the trees up to the point where they thinned. She canted her head as she took in the mountains, struck by their beauty as their white peaks met clear deep blue sky.

Winter was beautiful.

She always had loved this time of year, despite how hard her family tried to ruin it for her.

She could spend hours just standing in this one spot, taking in the forest and mountains, feeling nature surrounding her, and she was sure she wouldn't feel the cold. She tensed as a breeze swirled snow around her boots, caressed icy fingers across her face. Fine, maybe she would feel it.

She was already missing that hot chocolate she had left behind at Ember's. Maybe she should have brought the mug with her, could have been enjoying it right that moment as she took in the view. A thought pinged into her head. She could make herself a hot drink to stand on the deck with or bring back to this spot. It would keep the chill off her and allow her to spend more time out in the fresh air.

Holly looked over her shoulder at the cabin, tempted to head inside and make her own, aware that if she did she would end up curling up in front of the fire with it rather than coming back out to take in the view.

She looked back at the world around her. Just a little more time outside. The air would do her good and it was better than sitting indoors all day. Although, she might end up napping on the couch, worn out by the cold and the walk.

She stamped her feet to warm them and then set off again, following the concealed river to the other side of Cobalt's small territory, heading into the woods there. Animal tracks cut through the thin snow, stealing her focus as she picked out which species they belonged to, and mused over ones she didn't recognise.

Holly lifted her head and stilled as she found herself in a part of the woods she didn't recognise.

When she had first arrived, Cobalt had warned her not to stray too far north of the Creek, had told her scary stories about the bears there when everyone had been drinking beers around the fire Rath had built in the clearing, close to Ember's home.

Storm had assured her that she could wander all she wanted. The bears who remained at Black Ridge slept through the winter like their animal counterparts. It had reassured her, but only a little. Her walk back to Cobalt's cabin in the pitch dark had been swift, and she had made sure to lock the door behind her. Her mind had run wild that night, filled with fantasies about running into one of the bears, ones that had turned to nightmares.

Mostly because Rath had told her to get her butt straight back to the Creek if she ever crossed paths with any of the bears.

Or yell for help.

When she had looked at the others, none of them had contradicted him. Everyone had looked grave.

Holly had decided not to stray far from Cobalt's cabin, to keep firmly away from the bears' territory. She was sure they were all sleeping just as Storm had said, but she didn't want to risk it. She didn't want any trouble with them.

A bird flitted overhead and she turned and lifted her head to track it, raised her hand to shield her eyes as she tried to see it. It was long gone, disappeared into the trees.

She had been trying to catch sight of birds for days now, had only heard them so far.

A sudden sensation that something wasn't right hit her, had her instincts rushing to the fore, flooding her with awareness of the world around her.

Holly's spine stiffened.

She wasn't alone.

Her breathing slowed as her senses sharpened, as she listened hard for a sign that she hadn't imagined that someone was out there.

Watching her.

A bear?

Panic was swift to set in, the tales the brothers had spun about them filling her mind, making her heart race.

She did exactly what her alpha had told her to do.

She hurried back towards the cabin.

Prayed to the gods that whoever was out there, they wouldn't chase her.

Her heart jolted into her throat as a twig snapped behind her.

CHAPTER 3

The urge to follow the cougar female was strong, had Saint rising to his feet, taking a step in the direction she had gone. A branch snapped beneath his boot and he cursed as she broke into a run, found the strength to deny the instinct she ignited in him—an urge to chase down his prey and not let it escape.

Saint huffed, his breath fogging in the air, and forced himself to turn away instead. No good would come from scaring the female. He was too tired for a fight with the cougars, just wanted to sleep. He knew what the noise was now, so he didn't need to start a war.

He just needed to crawl back into bed.

He reached the edge of the woods, grumbled under his breath as he started wading through the snow, back towards the heart of Black Ridge. The sight of smoke drifting into the air from the firepit in the centre of the clearing was a welcome one, had him veering away from his cabin and heading towards it instead.

Knox and Lowe sat on the thick logs they had uncovered, ones set around the large firepit, a ridge of snow surrounding them to create a circular clearing around twenty feet across. Two entrances had been cut into the wall of snow, one leading to a path the twins had cleared to his cabin and one to their own homes. Branching off from that path was another one that led to the outbuilding that stood between his cabin and those of the twins.

Knox grunted as Saint sank onto the log opposite him, jerked his chin slightly and went back to prodding the fire with an iron, a sour look on his face. He was dressed more appropriately now, had donned the same warm protective gear as his brother wore, and both males had pulled thick black knitted hats on, covering their blond hair. Firelight flickered in his blue eyes as he stared at the flames, sitting hunched forwards with his elbows resting on his knees and his back to his cabin.

Beside him, Lowe sat upright, stifling another yawn. Two shovels had been propped against the other end of the log he sat on, and Lowe had removed his gloves. He leaned forwards, warming his hands on the fire, and looked over the flames at Saint.

"Cougars?" His deep voice was a rumbling growl, laced with fatigue.

Saint nodded. "They seem to be overwintering at the Creek this year."

Knox muttered something beneath his breath and Saint could feel his mood degenerating, turning blacker.

He pinned his blue eyes on Saint. "Why? What the hell are they doing there? They know we're sleeping here."

Lowe just looked at his brother and placed his hand on his back. He had never been the talkative one out of the twins. Knox said enough for both of them.

"There's some kind of celebration going on. I heard Rath ask Cobalt about a certificate, and the male said something about being ordained." Saint rested his elbows on his knees and stretched his hands out towards the fire, almost moaned as the heat of it chased the icy numbness from his bones.

Knox grunted, "Sounds like a wedding."

"Makes sense." Saint rubbed his hands together, warming them further. "Two of their mates are human. They probably wanted a traditional wedding ceremony to go with their mating."

"We still owe Storm and Flint," Lowe growled, and the cougars must have really pissed him off by waking him up because it *really* wasn't like Lowe to be out for blood.

"Believe me, I know that." Saint remembered all too well what those two brothers had done to him, but getting into a war with them wasn't going to change the past.

Although, it would probably improve his mood.

His bear side had been restless since Flint had rolled into the Ridge to pick a fight, wanted a rematch with the cougar.

He tried not to listen to that tempting voice inside him that said he could have revenge, and in the process teach the cougars a lesson for waking him and his kin from their winter sleep. His bear side had a tendency to make bad decisions if he let it take the helm, ones that usually got him into a lot of trouble and landed him with a whole heap of regrets.

"Saw a female in the woods too." Saint lifted his head and debated whether to say much more than that, some part of him growling at the thought of sharing her with Knox and Lowe, making him want to clam up and keep her to himself. He managed to shake off that urge as Knox sat up, giving him the whole of his attention. "Black hair. Petite. Grey eyes like the rest of them. Definitely cougar."

"Black hair?" Knox rubbed his blond beard. "Sounds like Cobalt's mate. I saw them from the other side of the river in summer."

Acid scoured Saint's insides as he thought about the fact the female belonged to Cobalt. It was what he had thought, but for some reason hearing Knox confirm that she was mated to another had Saint on the verge of shifting, made him want to roar and unleash his fury on everything in his path.

He pinched the bridge of his nose. Rubbed it. He was just tired and cranky. Just wanted to sleep.

"Did she cross into our territory?" Knox's voice held a dark note, one that warned Saint his thoughts were treading dangerous paths. "We could get some payback. The cougars messed with us. We mess with the cougars."

Tempting, but he tamped down his desire to let anger steal control of him, pulled back on the reins and cleared his head, refusing to let his bear side rule his actions. He wanted a fight right now, and it would be all too easy to let that part of him take the helm. Maintaining the peace between his pride and the cougars was more important than revenge.

Especially when only three of them were here and there were four cougar males at the Creek.

While he, Knox and Lowe would have the advantage of brute strength, the cougars were quicker, worked well as a team, and they were cunning too.

He dropped his head into his palm. And he really just wanted to sleep.

"I'll get some food on." Lowe stood, grabbed the shovels and went back to his cabin, taking a detour via the small outbuilding they used as a larder and storage room.

Knox continued to poke at the fire, showering sparks into the cold air, his expression slowly darkening. Saint could practically feel his mood taking a nosedive as the seconds ticked by, as they rolled into minutes and then close to an hour.

Evening was beginning to fall as Lowe emerged from his cabin, three bowls in one hand and an old cast iron pot in the other.

Saint's mouth watered at the smell of the food as Lowe sat on the log, set the pot down and pulled the lid off. Lowe filled a bowl with the hearty bean and beef stew, and held it out to Saint.

"Thanks." Saint was quick to take it, to grab the spoon and dig in. He groaned at the taste of it, threw Lowe an appreciative look.

"That good, huh?" Knox grabbed the next bowl from Lowe and scooped up a mouthful, ate it and was quick to nod. "Damn, that *is* good."

Lowe looked as if he might blush.

It was probably just hunger talking, making the stew taste like the most amazing thing on the planet, but then again, it probably wasn't. Lowe was a demon in the kitchen, always kept everyone well fed.

Saint polished off a second bowl and set it down on top of Lowe's one inside the empty pot. He stretched and yawned, tilted his head back and stared at the Milky Way that arched above the moonlit mountains. That was beautiful. Not the snow. Seeing the heavens so clearly because of the cold, still air almost made being awake in winter worth it.

Almost.

"I'm hitting the sack." He patted his full stomach. "Got enough fuel to see me through to spring now. Don't stay up too late."

Lowe nodded.

Knox snarled as a rowdy cheer went up to the south of the Ridge, followed by a round of laughter.

Saint glared in that direction, fisted his hands and fought to leash his mood as it blackened again, as he realised getting sleep wasn't going to be as easy as it had sounded just a moment ago.

Knox stood when another peal of laughter drifted through the trees.

Saint held his right hand out towards him, stopping him from moving, and Knox scowled at him but obeyed his silent order to remain where he was.

"I'll handle this. I'll speak to Rath, convince him to keep the noise down." Saint zipped up his coat again, the thought of having to head back out through the snow, in the dark this time, when it was even colder now, turning his mood pitch-black.

He had thought they would all be able to sleep now they knew who was causing the noise, but the look on Knox's face said the male wasn't thinking about hitting the sack. He was thinking about starting a war. No way Saint could sleep knowing that Knox was probably plotting ways to force the cougars to be quiet, liable to go off half-cocked to bloody some noses and ruin the fragile peace between Cougar Creek and Black Ridge.

He wanted to growl, his bear instincts coming to the fore as sleep was snatched from him again. He should have talked to Rath earlier, but he had wanted to avoid a conflict. Now he had the feeling that wasn't possible.

Either he told the cougars to turn down the volume of their celebration or Knox was going to tear through Cougar Creek on a rampage.

Saint followed the path he had cut through the snow to reach the fire when he had returned from Cougar Creek, his anger rising with each step that brought him closer to the cougars' territory. He was careful as he reached the woods, silently picking his way through the trees, moving with stealth so the felines wouldn't sense him until he had located Rath.

He lifted his head and scented the air, picked up the cougar alpha's familiar smell, together with the faint aroma of sweet berries. He growled at that scent, at the need to shift that swept through him in response to it, his thoughts treading dark paths of revenge again. Saint reined in that urge, put a lid on it and focused on his mission.

Talking to Rath.

The male was reasonable ninety percent of the time. If Saint asked nicely, explained the situation without a bite in his tone, then the male would probably agree to keep it down.

He tracked Rath's scent and frowned when it led him towards the mountains, not towards the clearing. Laughter rang through the trees in the direction of that clearing, voices there filling the night air, drawing his focus to them. Was the female there? Ember. Knox had said that was her name.

And that she belonged to Cobalt.

Saint's bear side growled at that again and he put it down to an urge to have revenge on that male for the part he had played in a fight that had ended with Saint gaining a scar that cut across his left eye, from his forehead to the start of his beard, as well as deep scars on his right shoulder.

He stalked through the trees, ditching moving stealthily when he sensed three males ahead of him. When he rounded a bend in the path, he spotted a cabin on the right hand side of it, and the three cougars on the deck of it. He recognised both Cobalt and Storm as the two with Rath.

While Rath had dark hair, his two younger brothers were closer to blond, with Storm's short hair a sandy brown colour and Cobalt's nearer to platinum. Storm was the biggest of the three by far, his broad build unmistakable as he stood halfway up a ladder Cobalt was holding, stringing up coloured lights on the front of the cabin.

Rath stilled at the same time as his brothers, his grey eyes swinging towards Saint as he prowled towards them, emerging from the shadows. The big cougar male slowly set the box he had been picking through down near a lamp on the deck and stepped off it, onto the path.

"Saint." Rath nodded, a frown etched on his face as he moved to stand a few feet in front of the cabin, placing himself between Saint and his brothers.

Always the alpha. Always taking care of his pride and keeping them safe. Rath was a good male. He would do the right thing, or Saint would convince him to do it.

Saint flicked a glance at Cobalt as he turned to face him and Storm as the male dropped to his booted feet beside him, and then set his gaze back on Rath.

"You mind keeping it down a little? Some of us are trying to have our winter sleep." Saint held Rath's gaze, ignoring the two younger cougars as they moved as one, coming to the edge of the deck.

Attempting to intimidate him.

The more rational part of him—the more human part—ignored their threat, uninterested in starting a fight with them and sure Rath wouldn't let it get that far. He would keep control of his brothers and keep the peace.

The side of him that was ruled by his bear instincts growled, had him gearing up for a fight, assessing the brothers to decide which to deal with first.

"Sorry—" Rath started.

"Not sorry," Storm snarled and jerked his chin towards Saint. "Fuck this guy. I got to remind you that he tried to kidnap Gabi?"

Rath looked over his shoulder at his younger brother and Saint could almost see him changing his mind, knew in that instant that the alpha was going to side with his brothers when he had looked ready to agree to keep the noise down before Storm had spoken.

As much as Saint hated admitting he had been wrong, as bitter as it tasted on his tongue, he lined up an apology about what he had done with Gabi, intending to explain the reason he had been in such a bad mood and that he had never intended to do anything to hurt her, had only meant to scare her a little to make her talk and confess whether she was a hunter or not.

He didn't get a chance to issue that apology or explanation.

Cobalt growled and stared Saint down, a flicker of gold emerging in his grey eyes. "You know you almost killed Flint. He would've been dead if it wasn't for Yasmin. You deserve fuck all from us."

Guilt gnawed at Saint's gut upon hearing that, the regret that had flared inside him upon thinking about his actions with Gabi increasing tenfold as he thought about his fight with the cougar male. He hadn't realised Flint had been injured that badly. He amended his apology, adding one about Flint too, and opened his mouth to let it tumble from his lips, sure it would be enough to convince Rath and his kin to be a little more considerate about the noise.

Storm spat on the ground near Saint's boots and glared at him.

Saint's bear side roared to the fore, wrenched control from him in a heartbeat as anger surged through him, had a growl rolling up his throat and fur rippling over his skin.

"Your brother came to Black Ridge to pick a fight. He got what he deserved." Those words came out as a vicious snarl, heavy with the rage that curled through him as he thought about that fight, as he thought about how the cougar had violated his territory—and his balls.

And now he and his brothers were violating the sanctity of his winter sleep.

"Yeah, and now you're getting what you deserve." Cobalt dropped off the edge of the deck and squared up to him, and the temptation to put the cougar in his place was strong, had Saint close to slamming a right hook into his pretty face.

Saint looked at Rath, sure he would have something to say.

Sure he would be the reasonable one out of the three and do what was right.

Rath just looked at his brothers.

Saint roared at him as he said nothing, as he turned to face him again and stared at him in the same way his brothers were, silently giving him his answer.

He wasn't going to order his pride to keep the noise down.

He wasn't going to be reasonable.

Saint forced himself to turn away, the jibes Storm and Cobalt threw at his back rousing his anger to new heights, until his blood thundered in his veins and his bear side overruled the human part of him, clouding his thoughts and pushing them down a single path.

If the cougars weren't going to be reasonable, then he wouldn't be reasonable either.

He strode through the forest, picking up speed as his mind churned and he seethed with a need to make the cougars pay. Fur rippled over his skin again beneath his clothes, his bones aching as his muscles coiled tight.

If they wouldn't let him sleep, then he wasn't going to let their celebration take place. He would find a way to ruin it somehow. His thoughts blurred, a mash of ideas that tangled together as he growled, as his fangs elongated and a need to shift ran through him. Pleasing images of turning back and fighting the three males filled his mind, had him losing awareness of the world as he sank into them.

He snarled as the hairs on his nape rose and his senses sharpened, yanking him back to the present.

He looked around himself, expecting to find himself back at the Ridge.

Stared at the raised cabin at the top of a small clearing.

A noise off to his left had him shrinking back into the shadows. His heart drummed harder, blood pumping faster and hotter as a familiar figure exited the trees just a short distance from him, humming to herself.

She looked up as the first flakes of snow began to fall, lowered her head and tugged her hood up as she wandered towards the cabin, heading straight past Saint.

Oblivious to him.

Deep brown fur rippled over his skin as he smelled her.

Sweet berries.

Laced with Cobalt's scent.

Instincts roared to life inside him, stole control of him before he could yank back on the reins.

Saint launched from his hiding place.

And snatched her from behind.

CHAPTER 4

Holly tried to scream as someone grabbed her from behind, but a strong hand clamped down on her mouth, pressing her black scarf to her face and smothering her. Her legs flailed as he lifted her, waves of tingles rushing through her as her heart started at a pace, as her mind struggled to process what was happening.

Trees swept past her as the male hauled her backwards into the forest.

Her eyes widened as she watched them disappearing faster and faster into the distance, as she heard the deep huffing snarl of the male who had grabbed her.

Her mind came back online in a flash.

She kicked her legs out, bucking her body forwards with each lunge of her feet, slowly wriggling free of his grip. He put an end to that by banding an arm around her stomach, crushing her lungs as he pinned her back against his front. She fought harder, refusing to give up, refusing to let the male take her.

A bear.

He had to be a bear.

All the tales the brothers had told her about their neighbours collided in her mind, filling it with terrifying images of what this male might do to her.

Rather than making her shut down and shrink away in fear, it only made her fight harder. She kicked at his knees with her heels, battering them whenever he took a step. He grunted as his right one gave out and he went down, dragging her with him. A root jabbed into her right side through her coat and she grunted too, the sound muffled by his hand and her scarf. She struggled to breathe and found she couldn't with the material pressed against her nose.

Panic finally set in.

She wriggled, managed to jimmy her left arm free and hit the male in the gut with her elbow. He didn't even grunt. He certainly didn't release her. She struck again, winced when her elbow hit a stomach as hard as a rock. Realising she wasn't going to escape him by hitting him, she took hold of his hand that covered her mouth, scratched and clawed at it as she tried to prise it away from her face.

He pulled her onto her feet, twisted with her and began walking forwards instead, each long stride jostling her as she wriggled and kept scratching at his hand. Her head fogged, thoughts blurring as oxygen became an issue.

Rather than trying to get his hand off her face, she pulled at the dangling lengths of her scarf instead, managing to tug it from beneath his hand. The second the thick material was clear of her nose, she breathed deeply, savouring each one as her head cleared, strength returning to her limbs as oxygen flowed into her blood.

She summoned that strength, focused on her body so she was ready to shift the moment she had enough.

Pulled down another breath.

Her head fogged again as his scent hit her.

Earthy, with a hint of cedar and snow.

Something primal inside her fired to life, had a growl rumbling up her throat and made her restless, but it wasn't a need to fight him she felt.

Holly locked up tight, too stunned by the heat that had ignited in her veins to do anything but hang limp in his arms, breathing in that scent in a desperate need for more, as if she couldn't get enough of it. The urge to shift dropped away, the thought of fighting him replaced with something infinitely more frightening.

They reached the edge of the woods and she spotted cabins in a clearing, a lone one to the right of the fire and two near the forest to the left of it.

The bears' territory.

A need to fight obliterated the primal hunger that had swept through her as the male carried her towards the lone cabin. She growled against his palm as she kicked his legs, snarled in frustration when he evaded each attempt to take them out again.

The desperate urge to fight grew stronger as two males who sat beside the fire stood and eyed her. They were strikingly similar. Twins, if she had to guess. She didn't like the way the one on the left looked at her, his face darkening as firelight flickered over it.

The one on the right took a step towards her, or at least the male who was holding her. "Have you lost your mind?"

"Back off," the brute behind her growled, his deep voice rolling like thunder across the land and shaking her deeply.

What he said next shook her deeper still, had blind panic rushing through her.

"I have plans for the female."

Plans?

Her eyes widened and she threw a pleading look at the one who had spoken, fought with all her might as the one who held her marched her up a set of steps to the deck of the lone cabin. The blond male looked as if he wanted to say something, wanted to do something, but the one beside him grabbed his arm and he looked at him instead.

That bastard shook his head.

Holly yelled against the palm of the male who held her, her words muffled by it, and lifted her legs to brace her boots against either side of the doorframe as she came within reach of it. She pushed hard against it, refusing to let him get her into his cabin. He growled and twisted with her, so she was facing the woods again, and her breaths came faster as he hauled her backwards into the cabin.

She angled her feet outwards, desperately tried to hook the toes of her boots on the doorframe, growled when she managed it and the bear easily kept on pulling her into the cabin.

Holly reacted on instinct.

Bit into his palm.

"Son of a—" He turned and tossed her into the cabin.

She cried out as she slammed into a worn brown couch, bounced off it and hit the wooden floor, catching her right elbow on the small coffee table and landing on her back.

Bear loomed over her, darkness reigning in his deep chocolate eyes as they narrowed, the left one tugging on a scar that intersected his eyebrow and continued down his jaw to the thick mass of beard that covered the lower half of his face.

Holly scrambled backwards like a crab, heart thundering and breath rushing from her.

He glared down at his palm and then back at her.

Bear yanked his hat off, revealing shaggy brown hair and the scar that continued upwards on his forehead. He tossed it aside and his coat followed it, and Holly was quick to dive behind the end of the couch furthest from him, placing it between them.

Fear tried to seize control again but she breathed through it, scowled at the brute and kept her focus on him, even as her eyes darted around the cabin, never straying from him for more than a heartbeat.

There had to be a way out.

Maybe if she screamed loud enough, her pride would hear her.

That thought went out of the only window when the bear advanced on her, a six-seven formidable wall of muscle packed into a black and green checked fleece that hugged impossibly large biceps.

His arms flexed as he clenched his fists and a drop of blood squeezed from between his fingers. She stared at it as it fell to the floor, as it splashed onto the wooden boards, losing track of the world as a strange need came over her. She breathed deeply, caught his scent and growled as it roused a need to fight.

Bear cocked an eyebrow at her. "Threatening me now?"

His deep baritone rolled over her, sending a thousand arcs of electricity tripping over her skin.

She hadn't been threatening him, but it was better he read it that way than interpret her growl in the right one. She had the terrible feeling her cougar side hadn't meant it as a threat at all. It wanted him. *She* wanted him. Oh gods, this couldn't get any more messed up. She had spent years feeling she was dysfunctional and doomed to a lonely life, and now every inch of her was on fire for a male who had kidnapped her.

There was something seriously wrong with her.

Her body locked up tight as he stalked towards her, refused to move no matter how desperately she tried to run. She could only stare at him as he closed the distance between them, his eyes holding hers, filled with anger.

The brute shoved the hood of her coat back.

Her eyes widened and she braced herself, almost curled into herself and away from him, but stood her ground at the last second.

Mostly because he suddenly stilled.

Just stared at her.

Her heart slowly settled as she stared right back at him, her breathing coming easier and her muscles loosening enough that she could probably make a break for it without tripping on her own feet.

Only she couldn't move.

She stood as frozen as he was, and she didn't like it. She didn't like how her gaze refused to leave him or how her blood quickened at the sight of him, at the scent of him.

She didn't like the fact she couldn't seem to bring herself to attack him.

"Why did you kidnap me?" she bit out, feeling a little braver as he continued to just stand there, showing no sign that he wanted to hurt her.

He didn't answer her, just raked a slow look over her that heated her blood. Panic. That was what was making her hot all over. Not that leisurely once-over he was giving her. Not that look in his eyes that screamed he liked what he saw.

He reached for the zipper of her dark purple jacket.

Holly slapped his hand away, hitting it hard enough that her palm stung, and was quick to move, placing the couch between them again.

His dark eyebrows pinched hard and he advanced on her, trying to close the distance between them again. She refused to let it happen this time, kept on moving at the same pace as he was, circling the couch.

Realising she had passed the damned door and for some damned reason hadn't made a lunge for it.

Bear growled and went over the couch, and she shrieked as he grabbed her and twisted her towards him. Holly hit him with everything she had, managed to gain enough room to clock him pretty hard in his face with her fist. He grunted and growled, banded his arms around her and hauled her against his chest.

"Settle down."

His deep voice rolled over her again. Lush. Warming.

She pushed through that weird haziness she felt whenever he spoke and kept fighting him.

"What do you plan to do with me?" She shoved against his chest, kicked him in his instep and weathered another rumbling growl.

She kicked again, missing her target this time. Her foot landed behind his just as she shoved him with all her might, as he went to adjust his grip on her. Her eyes flew wide as he lost that grip on her and toppled over the back of the couch, hit his chin on the cushion and his shoulder on the coffee table.

He snarled.

Shook his head as he shoved his palms to the floor and pushed back onto his feet.

"I just want to sleep," he growled, his face darker than ever as he flicked a glare at her. "I asked nicely."

"Sleep then," she barked. "But you're not sleeping with me!"

She dodged him when he sprang at her, stumbled into the kitchen and grabbed a heavy skillet from the stove. She twisted as she sensed him behind her, grimaced as she swung and smashed the flat of the cast iron pan into the side of his head. He staggered to his left and sank against the counter, his left arm resting on it to support him as his knees buckled.

Blood trickled down the right side of his head.

Holly ran for the other end of the room as he growled, cursed herself again when she realised she had gone straight past the door. What was wrong with her?

"I *was* sleeping." His deep voice was a rumble of thunder, a warning that a storm was coming and she was going to get caught up in it, and it was all her fault.

She should have run out of the door when she had the chance.

Bear twisted towards her, his eyes as dark as midnight. "You damned cougars woke me up. You woke us all up."

He started towards her, each step harder than the last, shaking the floor, and she eased around the couch, refusing to let him grab her again. She neared the back of it, glanced at the door behind her to her left. This time, she was going out of it.

"I asked Rath to keep it down, but no…"

She paused as she realised something.

He slammed into her, seemed as startled by the fact she had suddenly stopped as she was.

"You took me hostage because you want to sleep? That's ridiculous!" She couldn't believe what she was hearing.

Her cougar instincts were strong at times too, made her do things that her more rational human mind wouldn't have, but she had never done something as crazy as this bear had when she was in the grip of those instincts.

Although right now, her cougar instincts were making her stand up to a male who had at least twelve inches on her and weighed more than twice what she did.

So maybe she did do crazy things when they were in control.

Like standing up to an angry bear.

Part of her had expected to shrink away from him, to cower and curl into herself and be afraid. Only she wasn't. Rather than frightening her, his aggression only stoked a fire inside her, one that had her squaring up to him despite the difference in their size.

Holly put it down to having three older brothers, all of whom were overbearing at times, aggressive just like this bear was. She had learned to stand up to them so they couldn't trample all over her, forcing their will upon her.

Now she was doing the same with him.

He made a grab for her.

She dodged backwards, nimbly leaping beyond his reach, something that ripped a frustrated growl and a black look from him, and was quick to round the couch, placing it between them.

"What's your great plan?" she snapped. "Swap me for sleep? All you've done is anger my alpha and my kin. They'll be coming for you."

They would be coming for him quicker if she would just remember to go for the door every time she passed it.

He snarled low. "Let them come. I'm banking on Cobalt trying to take you back."

Cobalt? She frowned at the bear as she pondered that. Why was he expecting Cobalt in particular to come for her? Because she was Ember's best friend?

Holly figured that made sense. Well, she wasn't going to wait for Cobalt to save her. She was going to rescue herself.

She eyed the door, a quick glance the bear didn't notice as he rounded the couch again, hitting the straight in front of the log burner. She eyed him too, ran her gaze over him from his wild, unkempt brown hair over a rugged face, to impossibly wide shoulders and a torso packed with muscle squeezed into a checked shirt, down to tree-trunk legs encased in winter pants and heavy boots.

As far as she could see, she was up against an older bear, one who had barked orders at the others and had been obeyed. Not a good thing. If she had to guess, she would say he was the alpha.

Which meant he was the star of half the stories she had heard over the last few days.

"Which one are you?" she said, refusing to whisper those words despite the growing fear she felt.

He puffed his chest out a little, his smile confident. "Saint."

Warmth rolled through her as he tipped his chin up, some deeply primal part of her purring at the sight of him, at how strong he looked as he stood like that. She shut it down and continued with her plan.

Her brothers always hated it when she found ways to belittle them when they were trying to trample all over her, when she acted as if she wasn't afraid of them or wasn't impressed by their chest-beating behaviour.

Holly pulled a face. Shrugged for effect.

"I don't know one bear from another in this pride. You'll have to tell me whether you're someone important." She raked her eyes over him and arched an eyebrow. Playing with fire, but she wasn't going to let him intimidate her. She was going to irritate him. "You don't look important."

He scoffed at that. "I'm the pride alpha."

She pretended to mull that over as she rounded the end of the couch, keeping him away from her. "So a pride alpha has resorted to childish methods of getting his way?"

He growled. "I'm not being childish."

Holly tapped her chin, holding her nerve as he stopped opposite her, his face rapidly darkening. "My kin didn't do as you wanted, so you took something of theirs to force them to do it. Seems rather immature to me."

Her heart shot into her throat as he vaulted over the couch and grabbed her again, an unwanted thrill chasing down her spine at the display of agility. Her pulse rushed in her ears as he dragged her against him, his grip on her right arm bruising, his face dark with anger as his lips flattened and his eyebrows met hard, narrowing his brown eyes.

Holly tipped her head back and stared up at him.

Breathed. "Saint?"

"Hmm?" His gaze fell to her mouth, darkened in a way that had nothing to do with anger.

A way that thrilled her.

"You're hardly worthy of that name." She pushed the words out, sure she would regret them. Irritation flared in his eyes but he didn't take them away from her lips. "You abducted me, and you're holding me prisoner, and for what?"

"Revenge," he growled.

She scoffed now, feeling bold as he continued to gaze at her mouth, as his grip on her slowly loosened, as if she had cast a spell on him and could control him. The thought she had some sort of command over this strong male heated the blood in her veins and was one hell of a power trip.

"Revenge? What did Rath and Storm ever do to you?"

His free hand lifted and he stroked two fingers down the scar that darted over his left eye. "Your kin gave me this."

He released her and tugged his shirt off together with whatever he wore beneath it, revealing far too much bare flesh dusted with dark hair.

He tossed the shirt aside and growled as he pointed to his right shoulder, to deep scars that cut a groove in his muscles. "And this."

Holly tried not to stare at his body, tried to pretend she didn't notice how the sight of all that honed muscle heated her blood in a way no man had before him.

"And it doesn't end there. You want to see the scars from where Flint tried to turn me into a fucking eunuch?" He reached for his belt.

Holly shrank back and averted her gaze, her heart jamming into her throat and hammering there as panic swamped her, the sudden switch in her emotions wrenching a gasp from her lips.

His hands stilled and then fell to his sides, and his voice was gruff as he growled, "It isn't wise to wake a sleeping bear, and Rath—*you*—did just that."

She wanted to apologise, wanted to tell him that she would have kept the noise down if she had known she would wake him, but the brothers had assured her they wouldn't.

She refused to let those words leave her lips though.

She refused to feel bad about any of this or what had happened to him. Not now that she knew who he was.

She didn't look at him, was too afraid to as her mind raced. "You're the one who tried to kidnap Gabi... and now you've succeeded in kidnapping me. She told me about the threats you made... how you were going to—"

Holly couldn't bring herself to say the words. Her pulse raced, her throat closing tightly as she thought about the threats he had made to Gabi, how he had said he would erase the smell of Storm on her, and fear broke through the wall of her courage, tore it all down.

Saint towered over her, radiating fury she could sense in him, rage that blazed in his eyes as her brow furrowed and she risked a glance at him, needing to know what he intended to do with her.

For a heartbeat, he looked as if he might do something, but then he grabbed her arm and shoved her towards a staircase, releasing her before she even had a chance to panic.

"Sleep," he snarled. "I need space to think."

When she didn't move, he growled at her. It carried a warning, one she knew she should heed, but she couldn't convince herself to move. She locked up tight, frozen not by his threat but by the glimmer of regret that shone in his dark eyes as he looked at her. Curiosity tugged at her as she stared into his eyes, making her want to ask him why he looked as if he wanted to apologise to her.

His shoulders shifted on a deep sigh and he averted his gaze.

She had the feeling he didn't only want to apologise to her. He wanted to apologise to Gabi too. Had everyone been wrong about him? She found it hard to believe they had been, but as she looked at him and mulled over what he had said, she got the impression he acted rashly when angered.

Did things he regretted when he had cooled down.

"Saint?" she started.

"Go to sleep," he grunted. "The alternative is sitting on the couch with me."

Those gruffly spoken words were enough to convince her to head for the stairs, but she had no intention of sleeping.

She trudged up the wooden steps, stopped at the first turn and looked back at him. He scowled at her and picked up the skillet she had dropped, slammed it down on the stove and raked his fingers through his overlong dark hair as he huffed.

He cast her a look, one that held a flicker of an apology, and then stomped to the couch and slumped onto it.

She crept up to his room, a plan forming in her mind.

She wasn't going to sleep.

She was going to escape.

CHAPTER 5

Holly's eyes popped open and she silently cursed. Falling asleep hadn't been part of her incredible plan, but the furs beneath her had been so warm, laced with Saint's smell, and the adrenaline had worn off as he had remained away from her, leaving her exhausted.

She had only meant to close her eyes for a second.

Anger directed at herself curled through her, heating her blood. She shouldn't have fallen asleep. She should have been hyper-aware of the brute who was holding her captive, not letting her guard down by dozing off on his bed.

His bed!

She cast a fearful glance around her, half-expecting to find Saint beside her on it, and breathed a little easier when she found she was alone. Her clothes were as she had left them, her dark purple coat still zipped up all the way and black weatherproof trousers slightly rumpled but still in place. Even her boots were still on her feet.

Saint really hadn't come up to her.

Maybe he was still in front of the fire. Still awake. For all she knew, she might have been asleep for only a second.

She shuffled to the edge of the bed and quietly stood, crept to the banister at the front of the loft space and peered down into the kitchen below.

Her eyes widened.

Saint was still downstairs, but not in any way she had expected.

This wasn't good.

She banked left, heading for the spiral staircase that led downwards to the ground floor of the small cabin. Stopped when she reached the final bend and stared past the very rustic and tiny kitchen that consisted of a handful of wooden cupboards and a worn wooden counter, to a major problem.

The six-hundred-plus pounds of massive grizzly bear sleeping in front of the door like a bizarre draught blocker.

Holly glanced at the window above the sink to her left, couldn't make anything out in the low light. Was it still snowing? How late was it?

Her gaze strayed back to Saint. Was he in a regular sleep or a winter one? She didn't know much about bear shifters, hadn't realised before coming to the Creek this winter that some of his kind liked to sleep through the colder months, much the same as their animal counterparts.

She eased down the final steps and edged towards the kitchen, careful not to make a sound. When she reached the cupboards, she peered out of the window, squinting into the darkness. The low light coming from the log burner behind her was enough to catch on the flakes of snow as they fell, dancing past the window as a breeze played with them.

The world was quiet as that snow gently fell. Maybe it was a winter sleep that had welcomed Saint into its waiting arms, had him curled up with his huge lower half wedged between the wall and the final kitchen cupboard, blocking her way to the door.

The warm light of the fire shone on his dense fur, highlighting it with gold. Rounded ears twitched as a log cracked, his long paler muzzle wriggling, and then he stilled again. She waited for the fear to come, sure she would be afraid of him now he was in his bear form.

Only it didn't.

She felt only fascination as she stood there looking at him, as she noticed the scar that cut through his fur on the left side of his wide face and darted over his eye, into the shorter hairs that covered his muzzle.

Holly dragged her gaze away from him and took in the room, seeking another escape route. The cabin was smaller than she had thought, and far more basic than she was used to. Cobalt's cabin had modern furnishings, including a brand-new kitchen and a very comfortable couch. She eyed the worn brown one before her, curled her lip at the dent in the far seat cushion that said at least one set of springs had collapsed, and the rip in the back of it.

She looked around for a ceiling light too, almost shook her head when she found only an oil lamp sitting on a rickety side table. Talk about rustic. Did Saint even have electricity?

His coffee table looked as if he had made it himself, the legs wooden posts as thick as her wrists and hacked at an angle at the top ends, where they had been shoved into the thick piece of wood that formed the surface of the table.

She crept towards the other end of the room so she could make it out more clearly in the low light, and wanted to huff when she checked the entire wall and found only logs and cupboards. No windows. Damn it.

Holly went back to the kitchen, careful not to wake the sleeping bear, and scowled at the world outside. The snow was falling faster now, the flakes bigger, and the wind was strong at times, catching the snow and driving it into the window. A storm was brewing.

She cursed again.

Visibility would be poor and the fresh snow would dampen all the scents in the area, masking them. It was going to make it difficult for her to get back to the Creek if she managed to escape.

Not only that, but the snow would cloak her scent too, and that meant the chances were high that Rath and the others would think she had been caught in the storm during her evening walk and had been forced to shelter somewhere.

She went back and forth as she watched the snow, as she checked out the window and found it was one that opened. There was a chance she could escape that way, might be able to make a break for it before Saint woke.

Holly didn't reach for the handle though.

She just kept staring at the snow as the wind whipped it past the front of the cabin, apprehension rolling through her. She was strong. There was a chance that she could make it through the storm and back to the Creek.

There was also a chance the cold would sap her strength and she wouldn't find it before she was too cold to move. She hadn't exactly been paying attention to the route when Saint had grabbed her. It would be too easy for her to get turned around in the woods and get lost.

Saint snuffled in his sleep, luring her gaze back to him. His muzzle twitched, fur rippling in a wave down his back.

Holly almost smiled.

Caught herself at the last moment.

She should be afraid of him. This was a show of power to deter her from attempting an escape and it was a good one, but there was a reckless, bold part of her that wanted to know what his rich brown fur would feel like if she pushed her fingers through it.

Would it resist her? Be hard to move her hand through it? Would it be soft? Coarse?

That same bold part of her wanted to know how he would react to her touch.

Would he snarl and bare his fangs? Roar to drive her away?

Or would he accept her hand on him?

His rounded ears flipped back and forth, and his nose wriggled. A low rumbling noise escaped him, almost like a groan, and he smacked his lips.

What was he dreaming about?

Holly tensed as she realised he wasn't dreaming.

He was waking.

She twisted on her heel and hurried across the floorboards, praying none of them would squeak and give her away, and rushed up the stairs.

That bold part of her hoping Saint would come to her.

CHAPTER 6

Saint was slow to shake off the heavy arms of sleep, his head foggy with the need to forget what he had felt and sink back into her waiting arms, into that delicious dream he had been having.

He blinked his eyes open instead, because he was sure the female had been close to him.

He lifted his head and looked around the room, but didn't see her anywhere. He drew in a breath and caught her scent, savoured it as heat rolled through him, pulling his dream to the front of his mind again. His mouth watered, hunger for a taste of her flooding him, filling him with a need to know if she would taste of berries as well as smell like them.

Gods.

That was a sweet torment.

Saint lumbered onto his paws and focused, summoning the shift. He gritted his teeth as his bones ached, as his muscles burned as some contracted while others lengthened, and rose onto his back legs. The fur that covered him swept away from his limbs, leaving naked skin behind, and then his chest and back, and finally his head. He grimaced as his nose shrank at the same time, his jaw and teeth moulding into new shapes, and shook his head as his ears shifted downwards and transformed.

The shift took only seconds, but each one was agonising, had him wanting to roar out his pain as his body morphed.

When he was back to how he liked to be, he staggered forwards, clenching his jaw as his stiff leg muscles stretched and refused to obey him. His fault for sleeping with his backside against a flimsy door that did nothing to keep the cold out.

He grabbed the bottoms of his long johns and pulled them on, scrubbed a hand over his face and huffed.

Fatigue rolled over him, beckoned him to close his eyes, but he couldn't. He was too deeply aware of the female as his senses locked onto her in his loft bedroom above him. Her rapid pulse drummed in his ears, her fast breaths breaking the silence. She wasn't asleep then. Had she been contemplating escape?

Or just contemplating him?

He pulled a deeper breath into his lungs and her scent was so clear she must have been in the room a moment ago. She was the reason he had awoken, her delectable fragrance rousing him from a deep sleep.

A dangerous sleep.

With the winter calling him and a storm raging outside, making the world quiet again, it would be easy for him to fall back to sleep and not wake until spring, not even if she clambered over him to reach the door.

Scratch that.

His body ached, hunger riding him hard. He would definitely wake if she was on him. Just the thought of her pressed against him was enough to have him growing aroused.

What was it about this female that made her affect him so deeply?

He crept up the stairs, eased to a halt at the top of them and stared at her, replayed every moment with her as he gazed at her where she lay on her side on the bed, her black hair spilling across his pillow, her slender body curled into a foetal position.

When he had seen her in the woods, he had thought her pretty enough, but when he had brought her into his cabin and pushed her hood back and seen her in the light, he had been forced to re-evaluate his opinion of her.

She was stunning.

Beguiling.

Her beauty stirred his blood, made him want to growl and take hold of her, and bend her to his will, until she submitted to him.

Saint forced himself to turn away from her, knew in his heart he wouldn't cross a line with her like that, but he was tired, on edge, and didn't trust himself. He had frightened her enough.

He trudged back down the stairs and sank onto the couch, tipped his head back and tried to sleep but it eluded him now.

He stared at the ceiling, at the spot where she was on the other side of it, unable to stop himself from focusing on her. He lost track of time as he gazed at that point, as her breathing and pulse steadily calmed.

He wished he could be like that.

Calm.

Her scent was driving him crazy though and he felt as if the cabin was too small with her in it, as if he would go out of his mind if he didn't get some fresh air. Her fault. She made him crazy, had him twisted in knots as he tried to purge her scent from his lungs and failed dismally.

He dragged a hand over his face.

Gods, he was sure she had been stood close to him while he had been sleeping.

Had seeing him in his bear form frightened her?

He chuckled softly at that. He doubted it. He drew his hand away from his face and looked at the bite mark on his palm that was healing now. The little female didn't seem afraid of anything, not really. She was a bold one. A brave one.

Which only made him admire her more.

Saint shut down that dangerous line of thought because no good would come of it.

She was mated to another and he had taken her as revenge.

He needed to remember that, needed to get his head on straight and shut down the unruly part of him that wanted her.

He shifted his focus to the world outside as he looked at the window to his left. It was dark, but not because it was night. Morning had come, but the storm was stealing what little light they got at this time of year. Snow whirled past the window, and his bear side growled at him to stay inside, where it was warm.

But he couldn't.

He needed air.

Space.

A moment to catch his breath.

Saint shoved to his feet, stripped off his long johns and tossed them aside as he went to the cupboards. He grabbed a pair of black trunks from one of the drawers and pulled them on, followed by his weatherproof trousers and then his black and green fleece. He grabbed a pair of thermal socks and his boots, sat on the end of the couch as he tugged both of them on, and then stood and snatched his black coat from the rack.

He paused at the door, looking back at the loft, his focus locking back on the female.

Outside, the wind slammed snow against the cabin.

He shuddered at the thought of going out there, of leaving this place, when all he wanted to do was climb those stairs, crawl onto the bed and tug her against him, moulding her body to his, holding her while he slept. That need pounded inside him, growing stronger with every beat of his heart, an irresistible urge that took all of his will to shut it down.

He pulled his coat on and opened the door, resisted the urge to slam it behind him as he stepped out onto the frigid deck of his cabin. His face twisted as snow blasted against his side, as he peered into the haze of it, just about able to make out the forest and the cabins to his right. If it continued like this, it would be another whiteout. He trudged down the steps to the path the twins had made in the snow—a path that was already covered in four inches of fresh powder.

Saint tugged his hood up and zipped up his coat, huddled into it as he marched along the path, veered right at the firepit and headed towards the two cabins nestled against the edge of the forest.

A light was on inside the one on the left, the older of the two buildings. Knox lived there alone now, but he and his brother had shared it once, before Lowe had decided they both needed some space. Lowe's newer cabin was a replica of the old one, a touch larger than Saint's own cabin but similar in style, with a raised deck covered by the extended pitched roof but two windows on the lower half, one on either side of the door.

Above that door, there was a smaller window that allowed light into the loft bedroom.

Smoke curled from the metal chimney to the left of the roof, was caught in the wind and swiftly merged with the constant flurry of snow.

Saint knocked his boots against the side of the steps up to the deck, clearing some of the snow off them before he ascended the few stairs.

He rapped his knuckles against the door and waited, looked back at his cabin, squinting at it through the snow as a need to go back speared him, had his mind filling with thoughts of the female.

When Knox didn't answer, he knocked again, harder this time, impatient to have someone guarding Ember so she didn't get ideas about escaping.

The door opened.

Knox rubbed the back of his hand across his eyes and then upwards, over the unruly wild waves of his dark blond hair. The male was already dressed, wearing weatherproof trousers and a thick black cable-knit sweater, and he had trimmed his beard too, leaving just a light scruff on the lower half of his face.

The fatigue in his stormy blue eyes and the fact he had washed up told Saint that Knox hadn't been able to sleep, had been finding ways to pass the time in his cabin and had run out of things to keep himself occupied so he had settled on some personal grooming.

Knox grumbled, "What's up?"

"I need you to keep an eye on Ember while I go for a walk." Saint looked back at his cabin, wanting to curse as the snow grew heavier, trying to steal it from view.

"A walk?" Knox arched an eyebrow at him as he leaned his right shoulder against the doorframe and peered out. "Have you seen the weather?"

"Walked through it, didn't I?" Saint growled and folded his arms across his chest, straightened his spine and made sure Knox got the message that he wasn't messing around. "I just need to work off some energy. Thirty minutes tops."

Knox looked beyond him to the snow. "It's dangerous. Weather is getting worse by the second."

He was aware of that, and appreciated Knox's concern, but it wasn't going to stop him. He needed to get some air and some space. Standing on the deck of his cabin wasn't going to be enough. He had to get away from the female for a moment and get his head on straight, and that was something he couldn't do with her scent taunting him.

"I won't go far. Just a few laps around the property. I'll stick to this side of the creek." Saint hated to compromise, but Knox was looking as if he wasn't going to agree to watching Ember for him, and he didn't like how long he had been away from her already. He didn't have time to argue with Knox about this, or ask Lowe.

He doubted Lowe would help him even if he ordered it.

He had seen the look the older of the twins had given him, had heard in his voice that he thought Saint had made a mistake by snatching Ember.

Saint was starting to feel the same way.

"Fine." Knox grabbed his black coat and shoved his arms into it, his face darkening as he zipped it up. He pushed his feet into his boots and stepped out onto the deck. "But if you turn into a popsicle out here, I'm not saving your ass."

Saint chuckled. "I'm sure I could rouse a shift if I get that cold."

Although there was always a chance he would be too cold to make it happen. He wouldn't be the first bear to die because he had left it too long before attempting a shift to keep himself warm.

Knox closed his door and stepped past him, and as Saint turned to watch him walking towards his cabin, a fierce need to growl and roar blazed to life inside him, born of the thought of Knox being near her.

Saint forced himself to take the steps down from Knox's deck and to walk away, heading in the opposite direction, past Lowe's cabin. The blind on the door twitched as he neared it, and Lowe stared out at him, a hard look in his blue eyes. The male still wasn't happy about this turn of events. He averted his gaze and huddled down into his coat as the wind blew against his back.

It swirled around on him and caught his hood, pushing it back and blasting snow into his face.

He growled and tugged his hood back up, yanked on the elastics to tighten it against his head and looked at the untouched snow ahead of him as he walked, picking up pace.

His pace began to slow as a feeling built inside him with each step, setting him on edge.

The greater the distance between him and the female grew, the stronger his need to return to her became.

He looked back over his shoulder at the hazy cabin.

And he had the feeling it wasn't because he feared she was going to escape.

CHAPTER 7

Holly woke with a start, the hairs on her nape rising as her senses locked onto someone standing over her. She opened her eyes and stiffened, scooted backwards on the bed to place more distance between her and the male.

Not Saint.

She blinked sleep from her eyes, struggling to shake its hold, and eased back a little more as she took stock. It was one of the other males she had seen when Saint had been bringing her to his cabin. Hope flared and then died, her first thought that it was the one who had looked ready to try to help her swift to fall away as she got a good look at him.

As her eyes met blue ones that were dark as he gazed at her, as he towered over her without saying a word. He didn't need to speak for her to feel the threat, to know he wasn't going to be as gentle with her as Saint had been. Darkness etched itself on his handsome features and the fear she had expected to feel when she had been faced with Saint last night was quick to come this time.

She backed away a little more. "What do you want?"

Her senses stretched out, making her feel like a fool as she searched for Saint, some part of her desperately hoping to find him in the room below. Nearby.

There was only this male.

When he said nothing, she hissed at him and bared her emerging fangs in a threat. She scrambled onto her knees and off the other side of the bed, placing it between them. He cast a look at it and then at her, and chuckled. She was well aware the bed wouldn't stop him from reaching her if he wanted to, but it was her only line of defence. She couldn't shift without shedding at least some of her clothes and she wasn't about to strip in front of this male, giving him the wrong impression.

"Where's Saint?" Her voice wobbled a little as she tried to reach further than the walls of the cabin with her senses and found nothing but silence. Not even a blip of a person or anything for that matter. She glanced to her right, to the small window, and watched the snow swirling past it.

Her heart started at a pace as she grew deeply aware that she was alone with this male.

"Saint's out." The male's deep voice was little more than a growl. "Seemed pretty irritated. You want to explain why my alpha needed to take a walk in a blizzard, cougar?"

"I wouldn't know. Have you tried asking him?" she snapped, her hands shaking as she glanced to her right, at the window again, and then the banister.

He slowly moved around the foot of the bed, each step measured, his gaze never straying from her as he put an end to thoughts of vaulting over the railing and making a run for it.

"Told me to look after you." Those words, spoken in a brusque tone with a hint of wicked light in his eyes, had her moving.

She leaped over the bed and ran for the stairs.

Shrieked when he grabbed her from behind, his arms locking tight around her stomach, crushing her lungs.

"Where do you think you're going? I'm not about to have my alpha mad at me because you escaped on my watch," he growled into her ear and she wriggled and kicked at his legs. He clucked his tongue. "Play nice now, little kitty."

Like hell she would.

Holly reared her head back and smashed it against his face, ripping a grunt from him. The scent of blood laced the air and his grip on her loosened, and she broke free, stumbled a little as she landed with one foot on one step and the other further down the stairs.

"You little bitch." He lunged for her.

She ducked beneath his wild swing and punched him in the groin.

Twisted and ran down the stairs.

Shrieked and drew up short as he dropped right in front of her, his landing shaking the floorboards.

His blue eyes flashed dangerously as he advanced on her.

"You give Saint this much trouble? No wonder he needed a walk. Surprised he didn't kill you." His grin was cold as it stretched his lips. "Don't expect me to be so nice, Ember."

She had been about to run, but locked up tight before moving a step as his words hit her.

"Ember?" She frowned.

He grabbed her while she was distracted, twisted his hand into her black hair and ripped a cry from her as he hauled her to him. She bumped against his chest, fought to ignore the pain in her scalp as her heart and thoughts raced, and focused her mind.

She brought her knee up hard between his legs and he released her as he doubled over.

Snarled. "You hit me there again and I'm going to get angry."

Holly made a break for the other end of the couch to him, not missing how she was replaying exactly what she had done last night, or the fact that this time she was terrified. She didn't have time to examine why she hadn't feared Saint as she feared this male, shoved it aside for later and focused on evading him as he hurled himself at her.

She nimbly leaped to one side, watched him sail past and land hard on the floor.

Made a break for it.

Ran right for the door she had ignored several times when doing this same dance with Saint.

She yanked it open and wind slammed against her, knocking her back, and snow blinded her, the bitter bite of it swift to chill her skin.

The male grabbed her from behind again. "Not a chance. Saint will kill me if you go running back to your mate on my watch."

"Mate?" Holly frowned and pieced something together. "You called me Ember earlier. You think I'm Cobalt's mate."

That was why Saint had talked about Cobalt coming to save her.

They all thought she was Ember.

Anger was swift to rush through her, heating her blood and boosting her courage. They had meant to take Ember from Cobalt, had wanted to hurt both her best friend and a male who was coming to mean a lot to her too.

Holly hissed and growled, wrestled against the male's hold and when he only tightened his grip, she lifted her feet and braced them against the kitchen counter and the wall.

Bears were strong.

But cougars were made for jumping.

She gritted her teeth and snarled as she kicked off, as she sent both her and the male flying. He grunted as he landed hard, as wood cracked beneath him and she landed on top of him, half of her expecting to go straight through the floorboards. The bear's grip on her went lax and she sprang from his arms, swiftly turned and brought her foot down hard onto his stomach. His legs and shoulders lurched upwards, his arms flying to his waist as he grunted.

"You son of a bitch!" She levelled another kick, striking him hard in his side, and leaped backwards when he made a grab for her ankle. "I'm not Ember. I'm her best friend... and you're going to pay for trying to hurt her."

She flexed her fingers, her nails transforming into short claws as a hunger to hurt the male shot through her, as thoughts of her beloved Ember being held as she had been, treated as she had been, darkened her mood.

Holly yelped as the male grabbed her leg and pulled, loosed a grunt as she slammed onto her back and the air exploded from her lungs.

Before she could muster the strength to move, the bear was on top of her, his legs pinning hers, his hands tightly clutching her wrists to hold them to the floor above her head.

She stared up into his blue eyes, her pulse pounding faster, her instinct to fight giving way to a desperate need to escape as fear rocketed through her. Thoughts of hurting him turned into nightmarish visions of him hurting her.

He tightened his grip on her wrists and she cried out as her bones ached, as fire lanced them. He opened his mouth to say something.

She shrieked again as the door beyond her head burst open, as snow blasted inside.

And a terrifying roar deafened her.

CHAPTER 8

Saint barely stopped himself from shifting and killing Knox as he grabbed the male by the back of his neck and hauled him off the female. She remained frozen to the floor in the position she had been, her arms stretched above her head, her wide eyes fixed on the ceiling.

He pulled Knox to face him and roared in his face, relished the way the male closed his eyes and shrank back, how he lowered his head. His heart hammered, each breath he managed to pull down feeling as if it wasn't enough air as rage burned up his blood, as his claws elongated and pressed into Knox's neck. He wrestled with himself, with the urge to put the male in his place in a more physical way, seconds feeling like minutes as he waged an internal war.

Eventually, he wrangled the hunger to shift and fight Knox under control, but only because he didn't want to scare the female more than she was already.

He turned and shoved Knox out of the door, roared at his back for good measure. Knox's shoulders tensed and then he made a fast exit, practically leaping from the deck to land on the snow-covered path.

Saint breathed hard, wrestling his rage back under control, aware he was probably frightening Ember with his display of aggression.

He looked down at her, couldn't stop himself from easing to his haunches beside her and checking on her. "You all right?"

Her wide eyes darted to his, the emerald bright against the stony backdrop of her irises, but she didn't answer him, didn't even nod or shake her head. She just stared at him, fear reigning in her eyes, stoking his rage.

The black need to hurt Knox.

"Stay in the cabin," he grunted and stood, stormed out of the door and slammed it behind him.

He kept his senses fixed on her as he strode across the clearing, his gaze locked on Knox's back as he hurried towards his cabin. The male flicked a glance back at Saint. Saint growled and bared his fangs, picked up the pace until he was running. He caught up with Knox before he hit the steps of his cabin, collared him again and ran up to the deck, and slammed his spine against the log wall near the door.

"The fuck were you doing?" he snarled in Knox's face, his claws punching holes in the male's jacket. The leash on his temper snapped when Knox didn't answer immediately, and he hauled the male towards him only to smash him back against the wall, rattling the entire cabin. "Answer me!"

"Not what it looked like. I would never—" Knox slowly raised his hands beside his head, his tone even as he said, "She tried to escape. Fought me. I stopped her. She punched and then kicked me in the balls. You try keeping your cool when someone is brutalising your junk."

Knox knew damned well that he wouldn't have kept a level head in that situation, that he had reacted badly when Flint had clawed him there.

"I tried to stop her again when she went for the door." Knox scowled. "She kicked off from the wall or some shit and next thing I know, I'm flat on my back and she's beating the shit out of me."

"Ember's a cougar. They have powerful legs. You didn't think of that?" Saint squared up to him, barely holding back his need to hit Knox, to pummel his face worse than the female had already managed.

Knox's blue eyes widened. "She's not Ember."

Saint stilled, calm suddenly washing through him as he frowned at Knox. "What?"

"She's not Ember," Knox repeated. "She told me herself. Got damned crazy when I called her that name. Ember's her best friend, and boy is that cougar pissed you wanted to take her from her mate. Damn near pulverised my kidney with her foot."

Knox dropped his hand to his left side and grimaced as he held it.

Saint just stood there, struggling to make that sink in. The female wasn't Ember, which meant she wasn't mated to Cobalt. But she smelled like that male. Both times he had seen her, it had been near that male's cabin.

"You're sure of this?" Saint frowned at his friend.

"Ask my kidney. What's left of it. I'll be pissing blood for a week." Knox shrugged when Saint scowled at him, silently telling him to be serious. "She said so herself."

"Could be lying." He mulled that over, not liking the possibility now that he had started thinking of her as unmated, now that the possessive side she had roused in him had begun viewing her in a new light. One that provided a lot of answers for the questions that had been crowding his mind since he had set eyes on her.

"To protect her mate?" Knox said, and Saint wanted to growl at him for making such a sensible suggestion, one that was entirely too plausible.

"One way of finding out." He released Knox and stepped back from him, cast a glance to his right at Lowe, where he stood on his deck, watching events unfold. "You two head up to the valley. Get the lodge ready. I want to move her there."

Far away from the Creek and her cougar kin.

It wasn't just his desire to move her to a safer place that had him sending the twins away.

He wanted some time alone with her too, time in which he intended to figure out who she really was and why she drove him so wild.

Why he needed her so fiercely.

He backed off, keeping an eye on Knox until the last second, aware that he wouldn't dare attack him if he turned his back but unable to stop himself from making sure it didn't happen. Knox looked as if he wanted to voice an objection, or maybe complain about his kidney some more, but then he looked at his twin and sagged against the wall of his cabin, still clutching his side.

Saint turned when he reached the steps, was quick to break into a jog, one that brought him back to his cabin in only a few seconds. He mounted the steps to the deck, relief pouring through him as he sensed the female was still inside.

Was she Ember?

Or had he really snatched that female's best friend?

He pushed the door open, issued her an apologetic look when she stiffened and whipped to face him where she sat on the couch, her pulse shooting off the scale.

He eased the door closed behind him and she went back to staring at the fire. Her hands shook as she rubbed them together and darkness curled through him, stoking an urge to go back to Knox and beat him up after all.

He tamped it down.

"Knox apologised for scaring you. He has a bad tendency to let his bear take the reins, is quick to anger if he feels someone is threatening his kin, but that's no excuse for how he handled you." He frowned when she didn't react to that and refused to look at him, kept her eyes locked on the fire. He sighed, deeply aware that Knox had really scared her, battling an urge to go and bash the male's head against the wall some more. Maybe even let her do it. It might make her feel better. "Knox… says you're not Ember."

He removed his coat and slung it over the hook near the door.

"Knox is an asshole and can go to Hell." She glanced at him, fire in her grey-green eyes. "And I'm not."

"Mind if I ask for proof of that?" He edged closer to her, tried to keep his body relaxed so she didn't pick up on his tension and get worked up again and fight him.

He liked his kidneys functioning and not pulverised, and really didn't want her to kick him in the balls either. Although he probably deserved the latter as much as Knox had.

"Oh, I'm sorry. I left my ID in my purse when you kidnapped me!" she snapped, her eyes growing greener as she glared at him.

Fine. So, trying not to get her worked up wasn't going to happen because she was already worked up, ready to fight him.

But she hadn't run when she'd had the chance. Why hadn't she run? Because of the weather, or because of something else?

She turned her profile to him and stared at the fire again, a mulish twist to her lips that almost made him smile, might have if the situation hadn't been so dire. She had courage, had stood up to two full-grown adult male bears, and he liked that spark of fire in her.

"Other ways of giving me proof." He sidled another step closer, reaching the end of the couch, narrowing the distance between them down to only a couple of feet.

She stiffened. Her eyes widened. A hint of fear coloured them.

"Not that sort of proof." He barely kept the growl from his voice as he realised the path her thoughts were traversing, blamed Knox and his heavy handling of her. The idiot should have known that pinning her to the floor would terrify her, would make her think things were about to go seriously south for her. He jerked his chin towards her. "Lift your hair."

She frowned at him, but did as he asked, twisting her mass of black waves into her fists and raising it. Saint prowled around the back of the couch, heart beating a staccato rhythm against his chest as he prepared himself, steeled himself for the fact she might be mated.

Only when he came to a halt behind her and gazed at her nape, there were no scars.

Not a trace of a claiming bite mark.

"You're not mated," he whispered, throat thick as he stared at her nape and tried to make himself believe what he was seeing.

She dropped her hair and he wanted to growl as she stole that beautiful patch of unmarked skin from his gaze.

"No shit," she bit out. "I'm not Ember."

"If you're not Ember, who are you?" He moved around the couch again, sure to head back towards the end nearest the door, just in case thoughts about escaping him finally popped into her head as her shock and fear subsided.

"Her best friend." She tipped her chin up and folded her arms over her chest, pulling her purple jacket tight across her shoulders.

So that was how she wanted to play it now. She had information he wanted and she was going to refuse to give it to him, was going to make him suffer for it because of what he had done, and what Knox had done.

Saint still wanted to growl at how the male had been handling her, pinning her beneath him.

He kept that need in check, not wanting to scare the female.

She slid him a black look. "I'm not sure how you mistook me for Ember. Ember is curvy, and pretty, and has blue in her eyes."

Saint gazed at her, couldn't have taken his eyes off her if he had wanted to. "So that's where I went wrong... I accidentally grabbed a beautiful female."

A hint of colour climbed her cheeks and she was quick to avert her gaze, and he wanted to growl and puff his chest out because he had been the one to make her blush.

"You're such an asshole," she muttered.

An asshole who had put a flush in her cheeks and a flicker of heat in her eyes.

"How come you smell like Cobalt?" He studied her closely, seeking the tiniest hint of nerves, trying to see if she was lying to him because he really needed to know the truth about this. Both sides of him had been angry when he had smelled Cobalt on her. Both sides of him had lost their minds at the thought of her with that male.

With any other male.

Her lips flattened and he thought she wouldn't answer him, but then she tilted her chin up and said, "I'm staying in his cabin while he and Ember share her one."

The darkly possessive part of him she had awoken didn't like that she had been sleeping in another male's bed.

Didn't like that Knox had been all over her and she smelled a little like him now.

She fidgeted again, her gaze downcast, the fire he had sparked in her fading as she toyed with her fingers. He felt the fear rising in her, heard it in her heartbeat, and knew her thoughts were traversing dark paths again, ones involving Knox.

"I'm sorry Knox got rough with you." Those words came effortlessly to him as he gazed at her, as a tight feeling formed in the centre of his chest, one that felt as if it wouldn't ease until he had calmed her and she was relaxed again.

Her tone was sharp, lashed at him as she bit out, "I don't like this game... sending that man in to do your dirty work."

Gods, how low she thought him.

Heat flared in his veins, had him taking a hard step towards her, one he regretted when she shrank back and her hands came up to her chest in a protective gesture that almost killed him.

He didn't want her to fear him.

But he had done a terrible job of giving her reason not to feel that emotion around him.

He shoved his fingers through his hair, trying to wrestle his feelings back under control, sure she was picking up on his agitation and anger towards Knox and reading it as anger towards her.

"I didn't send Knox here for that... Knox wouldn't have... He isn't like that. None of us are. I only asked him to keep an eye on you. I should have known it would scare you, and I should have known Knox would react badly if you tried to escape." He flexed his fingers, drew down a breath and calmed himself. That feeling came easily as he looked at her, right into her eyes, picking out every fleck of precious emerald against the silver of her irises. He sighed. "I wouldn't hurt you. I don't think I could hurt you."

Admitting that made him feel weak, strangely vulnerable as he stood before her, as part of him waited for her to say something while the rest hoped she hadn't heard that soft confession.

She glanced at the log burner and then the couch, and then the broken table, looking anywhere but at him. He smiled tightly, could understand her reaction. She didn't need to believe him. He was cool with that. He really was.

Part of him didn't believe it himself.

Not because he thought he could hurt her, but because it shook him and peeled back another layer, making the source of the instincts she triggered in him clearer.

Although he still wasn't quite ready to acknowledge where they came from.

Saint edged a little closer to her, mustered the courage he always seemed to need when he was around this petite, beautiful female, and eased down onto the arm of the couch, as close to her as he could get without scaring her.

"What's your name, best friend of Ember?" he husked, aching to know it, sure she would be able to see how deep that need ran if she would just look at him.

"If I tell you, you have to let me go." She glanced at him and lingered as their gazes collided. "You have no use for me. I'm not the one you wanted."

Gods, she was the one he wanted. She didn't know how fiercely he wanted her. It was taking all of his will not to tell her how beautiful she was as she gazed up at him, a softness in her eyes that he didn't deserve. It was taking all of his will not to slide down the arm of the couch and settle beside her, maybe even slip his arm around her waist and tug her a little closer if she didn't spook.

He wasn't good at this sort of thing, was deeply aware that if he tried either of those things, he would only make things worse, and he liked the calm that had fallen between them.

Liked that she no longer looked afraid of him.

Was relaxed around him.

He frowned as she rubbed her nose and he noticed it was red, and not because she had cried, because this female didn't seem to cry about anything, not even when a bear had scared her witless.

He looked at the log burner, his frown deepening as he saw how dim the light from it was now and noticed the chill in the air.

Saint stood, bent and picked up the broken pieces of his coffee table, keeping his motions smooth and slow, so he didn't startle the female. He rounded the couch, walking past her and keeping his senses trained on her. She showed no inclination to move as he headed for the far end of the cabin, as he set the pieces of the table against the wall there. He would have to make a new one come spring.

He grabbed a few of the logs from a stack on the right side of the burner and rounded the couch again, resisting the urge to cross in front of the female. She hadn't made a break for it. He wasn't sure whether that was a sign that she was starting to trust him or was because she wasn't foolish enough to run out into a storm.

Snow battered the window above the kitchen, covered the panes in the door too, and the wind howled around the cabin. Knox and Lowe were going to have one hell of a cold walk to the lodge, but they would make it. The route to it was through the forest, where they would have some cover from the weather.

He eased to his knees on the fur in front of the fire, soul-deep aware of the female close to him, how this position placed him only inches from her knees.

And yet she still didn't move. Didn't shrink away. Didn't lash out at him.

Her gaze remained steady on him, heating him by degrees, filling him with an ache to look at her.

Saint forced himself to focus on something other than that incredible pull to gaze at her, opened the door of the burner and placed two logs onto the fire, stoked it a little and then shut the door, latching it again.

The flames were swift to catch on the logs, filling the thick silence with the sound of their roar and the harsh pops of wood splitting.

"Maybe you don't have a name," Saint muttered to the fire, shivered as heat rolled down his spine in the wake of her eyes as she ran them over him.

The urge to growl was strong, but he denied it, clung to control so this calm between them would continue. He liked it. It felt right. Every part of him felt relaxed, both the man and the bear. He couldn't remember ever feeling like this, was sure he hadn't in a long time. There was always something playing on his mind, or his bear side was always agitated by something, but here in this moment of beautiful silence, with the female's eyes on him, with her close to him and her scent swirling around him, he felt only calm.

Only a sense that this was where he belonged.

That everything was right in the world.

"Holly." Her whisper-soft voice teased his ears and he started, tore his gaze from the fire and looked over his shoulder at her, needing to know she had just spoken and he hadn't imagined it. She cleared her throat a little. "My name's Holly."

"Holly." He rolled that name around his tongue, tried to see if it suited her. He liked it for her. She was sweet as a berry but could be prickly too, had a sharp edge to her that no doubt kept a lot of people at bay.

Although holly berries were bitter and toxic, while her scent was sweet and heavenly.

He waited for her to ask him to let her go, but she didn't. She just stared at him, banked heat in her grey-green eyes, warm firelight flickering over her face.

He refused to feel guilty about what he had done and why she was here, but that didn't stop him from feeling that emotion as he looked at her. Part of him wanted to take her back, the rest of him snarled to keep her. The cougars would have realised she was missing by now. Returning her meant admitting he had done something wrong and inviting a fight. He was done fighting them. They played dirty.

Saint sagged a little as he realised the real reason he didn't want to take her home.

He didn't want to let her go.

He didn't want this, whatever it was, to end even when he knew it would.

The cougars *would* come for her.

"What happened with the other bear?" she murmured and he sensed the trickle of fear in her.

"You don't have to worry about him. He's gone," Saint growled, his need to protect her rising to the fore again. "We're alone now."

She stared at him in silence.

Did she feel as aware of him as he did of her?

He moved to face her and resisted the urge to place his hand on her knee, aware that she would slap it away if he dared to touch her. Resolve flowed through him, roused by his need to protect her, and he hoped she would see it in his eyes as he gazed into hers.

"I swear, Holly... even if Knox wasn't gone, you don't need to be afraid."

He gripped his knees to stop himself from touching her as her face softened, as a tiny flare of warmth lit her eyes.

He growled low.

"I will never let anyone hurt you."

CHAPTER 9

Holly was doing her best not to be distracted, but Saint wasn't making it easy. She had been giving him the silent treatment, unintentionally at first when she hadn't been sure what to say in response to his growled vow to keep her safe.

A promise that had ignited heat in her veins and roused her cougar instincts, made her want to growl herself for some unnerving and unknown reason.

She had lost herself in trying to figure out what was wrong with her, why she kept reacting to Saint in ways she had never acted around others, and had been silent so long that the thought of speaking made her uncomfortable. There was too much pressure on her now, as if whatever she said would have to be incredible or inspiring given how long she had been silent.

Her gaze tracked him against her orders and she fell into drinking her fill of him. She was sure everything he was doing; it was done on purpose. He was trying to get her to look at him.

So far, he had removed his shirt and washed up in the sink, drying himself off with a small towel as he had been looking at her. His smile had been a little too satisfied when she hadn't been able to drag her eyes away from his chest, so she had flashed him her middle finger.

In response to that, he had dampened his hair, had grabbed a mirror and some scissors, and had taken to cutting his hair and trimming his beard.

Holly stared at the fire, trying to come up with a plan to escape and failing dismally as her focus drifted back to the mountain of a man just a few feet from her. He was humming a tune now.

"You want a drink?" His deep baritone rolled over her and through her, heating her blood.

"No." She made the mistake of looking at him.

That heat became an inferno and she cursed him for trimming his beard down to a short layer of scruff and taming his wild brown hair.

He was too handsome.

It was a little disarming.

Actually, it wasn't just a little disarming. She had been fighting softening towards him and now he had made it harder than ever to hold on to her anger. He was transforming before her eyes, becoming so different to the male who had snatched her.

Holly clenched her fists in her lap.

He *had* snatched her.

She was his captive.

That was enough to have her heart hardening again, to have her walls coming back up. He could be handsome all he wanted, could smile and be kind to her, but it didn't change the fact he had kidnapped her to hurt her friends and that he showed no sign of releasing her.

"I want to go home," she snapped, her mood taking a dark turn. Good. She clung to that anger, used it as a shield against him as he frowned at her, his rich brown eyes gaining something akin to hurt, as if the thought of letting her go pained him.

"No." He looked over his shoulder at the kitchen window. "You really want to go out there?"

She glanced at the window and lingered. The storm was worse now. Snow constantly rushed past the window, almost horizontal as the wind caught it. That wind whipped around and hit the glass, rattling it.

Fine. Maybe she didn't want to go out into the freezing blizzard.

As soon as it died down, she was making a break for it though.

"Fucking snow," Saint grumbled, deep hatred in his tone, as if he held it personally responsible for all that was wrong in the world.

"You don't like the snow?" She looked at the window and then at him, caught the black look on his face before he turned his back to her and stared out of the window too, his hands braced against the counter in front of him.

"Do I sound like I like it?"

"No." She twisted on the couch, angling herself towards him, curiosity gripping her. Was it a bear thing? Cougars weren't bothered by the winter, not as the bears clearly were. She didn't feel the call of the wild as Saint did, had no instinct to sleep through the colder months. "I was born in winter. I always liked the snow when I was younger, but not so much these days."

He frowned over his shoulder at her and came to face her, planted his backside against the counter and folded his arms across his very bare chest. Would it kill him to put his shirt back on now that he was done with the manscaping?

"Why don't you like it now?" His dark eyes searched hers.

She cursed herself for getting so comfortable around him, didn't want to answer his question but could see in his eyes he wouldn't let this one go. He wanted to know why she had changed her opinion of snow.

She sighed. "My family are a handful and always tease me at this time of year, making my life hell. This is the first time I've managed to escape them for the holidays, and look at what happens. I get myself kidnapped. They'll never let me leave again."

He was quick to avert his gaze, his mouth flattening as he turned his profile to her as if that would change what he had done. He pushed off and came to her, and rather than feeling tense that he was near her, she found herself wanting him to sit with her, to tell her more about himself.

He didn't.

He sank to his knees in front of the fire and tended to it. Holly studied his profile and the feelings her senses could detect in him, reading him like an open book. He felt guilty about his actions, yet he wouldn't let her go.

Why?

She doubted it was because of the storm and that he didn't want her freezing out there or getting lost.

Silence fell again as he stoked the fire, as the warm light of it danced across his rough but handsome features, attempting to soften the harsh planes of his face as he glared at it.

When that silence became too comfortable again, she searched for something to say.

He didn't take his eyes off the fire as he spoke. "Are you so young that you're not allowed to be away from your family? I'm not sure how cougars work. Are they like other shifters?"

Heat that had nothing to do with the fire scalded her cheeks as she realised he was trying to ask about her age and whether she had matured, was considered an adult now. Most feline shifter species reached maturity at around a century old when biological urges like desire and need awakened.

Together with the ability to breed.

She really didn't want to answer that question, but as she stared at the fire, avoiding his gaze now as he looked at her, it struck her that he had a point.

She was old enough to go her own way.

To do as she pleased.

She shifted her gaze to meet his, stared into his dark eyes and had the feeling that what she wanted to do was something dangerous.

Something wicked.

His deep brown eyes warmed, gained a shimmer of gold as he looked at her, his pupils slowly dilating. Firelight flickered across the broad expanse of his bare chest, tempting her to trace his hard muscles with her fingers, to know the feel of a male's body at last.

Apparently, she wasn't dysfunctional after all because whenever she looked at Saint, the urges she had thought she didn't possess roared to life, almost overwhelming her.

She pressed the back of her hand to her overheating cheek and stood, struggled to breathe as she muttered, "The fire is a bit hot."

His gaze tracked her as she moved away from him, towards the far end of the room, fanning herself with her hand as her heart raced.

And her cougar side growled, pacing restlessly, flooding her with a startling urge to turn that snarl on him, to walk right up to him where he knelt on the floor and stand over him, take hold of his jaw and keep his eyes on hers. Holly recognised that urge for what it was—a display of dominance.

Her hands shook, as unsteady as her breathing as that hunger rattled her.

"Holly?" Saint eased onto his feet in a sexy, fluid move that spoke of strength, had his muscles rippling in a symphony that came dangerously close to ripping a feral, possessive growl from her.

She was quick to shake her head, fanned herself more furiously. "I'm fine. Just… stay over there."

Because she wasn't sure what she would do if he came any closer to her.

Pouncing on him seemed the most likely outcome.

She breathed through the cacophony of instincts that were intent on ripping her apart, had her unsure of herself, made her feel as if she was looking at a different person. Not chaste, sweet Holly, who felt nothing when a male looked at her, couldn't even muster the desire to kiss one.

No. This Holly was far removed from that one. This Holly wanted to pounce on Saint and claw him, wanted to dominate him and make him submit to her, revelled and found pleasure in the thought of him doing just that.

"You don't look well." Concern shone in his dark eyes as she glanced at him.

"I just need some air." She looked around her, desperately seeking somewhere she could get that air. "Why do you have so few windows?"

She hurried to the kitchen, couldn't stop her feet from moving as she stared at the window there, as her temperature hit boiling point and she feared she was going to pass out if she didn't cool down soon.

She was panicking.

"Holly." Saint strode to the door, and she thought he meant to block it, that he would stop her from opening it and getting the air she needed, air that felt vital, the only way of stopping herself from passing out.

She growled at him and bared fangs.

He arched an eyebrow as he opened the door at the same time as she threatened him.

Shame flooded her cheeks with even more heat and she lowered her head as she scurried past him, relief crashing over her at the first cold kiss of the wind on her face. Saint caught her arm when she tried to step out onto the snowy deck, holding her back. She shivered at the firmness of his grip on her, at the strength she could feel in it together with a silent declaration that he wasn't going to let her go.

That did more to calm her racing heart and cool her burning blood than the air that swept snow against her.

Her temperature quickly took a nosedive back to normal, the strange urges that had seized control of her falling away as Saint held on to her arm, as she grew aware of him standing just inches behind her, his gaze on the back of her head.

"Better?" he rumbled.

She nodded, breathed slowly as she focused on him. Couldn't stop herself from speaking and filling the silence. "Cougars are like other shifters. I matured at just over a century old, but I still live with my family... for now. Ember has only just left her family and I want to do the same. I want to see more of the world."

Gods, it felt good to admit that out loud to someone, and to herself.

She really did want that.

He slowly tugged on her arm, pulling her around to face him. His dark brown eyes searched hers. "How much of the world do you have left to experience?"

He was good at that—asking probing and very personal questions without saying them directly.

He wanted to know how much experience she had with males, and that was one question she wasn't going to answer. She searched for a way to shift the course of their conversation.

Saint released her and rubbed the back of his neck, his expression grim as he grumbled, "I made you uncomfortable again. How about I apologise with a drink? I might have some hot chocolate."

Holly smiled, relieved she didn't have to evade his question, and tempted by the fact he had offered her favourite drink.

"That sounds nice." She pulled a face as an urge hit her, roused by the thought of sipping hot chocolate. "Maybe come back to it. I have a more pressing need than a warm drink."

He frowned. "What's wrong?"

She glanced around his cabin and cold washed over her as she realised something. There was only one large room and the loft. Only a single door in the entire cabin and she was stood next to it. Her eyes darted back to him.

"Where's the bathroom?"

Saint hiked his thumb over his shoulder, towards the back of the cabin. "About sixty feet that way."

Holly squeezed her thighs together and stared at the snowstorm as wind howled past the cabin.

She re-evaluated his home.

Rustic was too good a word for it.

She stared at Saint in horror, aware of how she was about to give away that she had no intention of escaping him while the storm was raging but unable to muster even a shred of concern.

"You can't seriously expect me to go out there?"

CHAPTER 10

Saint would have found the horrified look on Holly's beautiful face amusing had it not been for the awareness that beat in his veins, warning him that she found his home wanting, that it wasn't good enough for her. He braced himself, but was sure it would do nothing to deflect the anger he was about to feel.

Or was that hurt?

She cast another wide-eyed glance around her, checking every inch of his cabin, and then threw him another shocked look. "You're not kidding. You don't even have an indoor toilet!"

And there it was.

His pride took a direct hit and he growled at her, bared short fangs as she looked ready to launch another salvo at him. Her lips compressed and he sensed the fight in her, how fiercely she had to battle herself to stop herself from uttering another insult.

So his home was a little more basic than what they had at Cougar Creek. Who cared?

He turned his cheek to her as it hit him that she did. She cared.

And for some godsdamned reason that made him care too.

"The cabin is old," he grumbled, anger towards her swift to morph into anger towards himself. He didn't need to explain why his cabin lacked one of the most basic of facilities. He didn't have to explain anything to her.

Wasn't as if he wanted her approval after all.

"I can't pee out there in the freezing cold!" She tossed another disgruntled look at the open door, at the white-washed world beyond it.

Saint opened the cupboard to his left, close to the stairs, and pulled out a chamber pot. He regretted it the moment he offered it to her, as her wide eyes leaped between him and it, going back and forth so many times he was sure she was going to make herself dizzy.

"Good gods, no." She turned her nose up at it, and then some of her bravado slipped as she cast a glance at the outside world and her voice dropped to a hushed murmur. "I'll go outside because I'm not having you standing over me."

Saint shoved the pot back in the cupboard and kicked the door closed. "You'll have me standing over you either way. I'm not letting you out of my sight."

She glared at him, fire igniting in her eyes, bringing out the green. "Not a chance. I'm not peeing with you anywhere near me."

"It's the chamber pot or a sixty-foot trek through the snow. Be thankful Lowe cleared a path to the outhouse. Only other option is crouching in three feet of snow..." He looked out at the grey morning, at the snow whipping past the cabin. "Might be more by now. Might not even have a path to follow to the outhouse."

She pressed her thighs harder together, and he couldn't believe how seriously she was debating this, or how big a problem it was for her. All she had to do was cop a squat on the chamber pot or brave the weather. She was acting as if he was asking her to scale Mount Everest to reach a toilet.

"Sooner or later, Holly, you're going to have to go. You're not going to have a choice in the matter either. You really have so much pride that you would rather wet yourself?"

Her eyes widened again and she looked ready to hit him as a blush burned her cheeks.

She turned her profile to him and folded her arms across her chest, pulling her purple coat tight across her shoulders.

"Fine." She huffed and slid him a sideways glance. "Is there at least toilet paper in the outhouse?"

He frowned at her and went for his shirt, plucking it off the back of the couch. "We're not that uncivilised. Plenty of paper for your delicate parts."

He stilled with his arm halfway into his left sleeve and looked at her, suddenly aware of her again, of those feminine curves she hid beneath thick layers of protective clothing. Her gaze scalded his chest, heat back in it that said he wasn't the only one whose thoughts were rolling down dangerous routes.

Wicked routes.

When she looked ready to bolt out into the storm to escape him, he quickly pulled his shirt on and buttoned it, and closed the distance between them again. He reached over her, every fibre of him aware of how close she was to him, how she didn't move to distance herself, just stood there and let him be near her. He breathed deep as he grabbed his coat, savouring her scent of sweet berries, his mouth watering at the thought of dropping his head and tasting her lips.

He hadn't been born yesterday, knew that her complaint about the fire being too hot had been a flimsy excuse to cover what had really been happening to her. She wanted him. She wanted him with the same ferocity as he wanted her, only it frightened her.

Hell, maybe it frightened him a little too.

He had never felt like this around anyone before her—torn, confused, unsure what the hell he was doing, craving the feel of her eyes on him.

Hungry and wild for her.

She swallowed hard and twisted away from him, kept her gaze fixed on the storm as he pulled his coat on.

There was a tremble in her voice as she said, "Is it day?"

"It's day. Late morning maybe. Not going to get much lighter than this." He stepped up behind her, unable to deny the ache to be closer to her, to see how close she would allow him to get.

When he inched a little closer, she tensed, and then hurried forwards.

"Round the back, right?" She was quick to rush for the steps, and he chuckled as the wind caught her and she was forced to brace herself, was almost toppled into the deep snow.

Saint closed the door behind him and took hold of her arm, his grip firm. "Let me show you the way, my lady."

She huffed at him, but didn't make him release her, just accepted his hand on her. He kept her close to him as the wind battered them, as snow bit into his face and hands. She bent her head, muttering things beneath her breath he couldn't make out over the howl of the storm. Reaching the outhouse was slow going, and his fingers were numb by the time he spied it through the snow.

"That's a big toilet," she muttered, teeth chattering in a way he didn't like. She was getting cold too.

"It's a few things in one building. Larder. Storage. Bathroom." He tried to pick up the pace to stop her from freezing, only she didn't match his speed and he almost ended up dragging her along behind him.

"Gods!" she bit out as a particularly brutal gust of wind picked snow up and hurled it at both of them, plastering her front.

"Come on. Not far now." He pushed himself forwards, determined to get to the outhouse, because she wasn't the only one who needed to go to the toilet now. The cold had tipped him over the edge too.

"Lovely weather we're having." Her breezy tone made him smile.

"And now you know why I hate winter." He tucked her behind him as wind scoured the Ridge again, shielding her from the worst of it. He had to release her to keep her there, but any fear she would make a break for it disappeared as she fisted the back of his jacket, clinging to him.

"You make a good wind blocker." She nestled a little closer to him and muttered something about how warm he was.

She had to be freezing if she thought he was warm, because he was so cold that he was sure his balls were about to fall off.

"Why, thank you." He breathed a sigh of relief when he reached the wooden hut and tugged the door open. "Here you go. Door to door service."

He lifted his left arm and looked under it, wanted to smile again as she poked her head around him, but his face was frozen. She was quick to dash for the cover of the bathroom and even quicker to slam the door in his face.

Saint remained behind the cover of the building and relieved himself, made fast work of it as the cold chilled him. He tucked himself away and zipped up, moved back to the door and waited. When more than a few minutes had passed, he rapped his knuckles on it.

"What's the hold-up?" he grumbled. "It's fucking freezing out here."

Her soft voice came through the door. "I can't go... you'll hear me."

He scoffed at that. "I'm standing in a roaring blizzard. I'll hear nothing."

She muttered, "You will."

Saint rolled his eyes and searched for a solution, something other than offering to move away from the door because he wasn't going to leave her unguarded. "I can sing, then I won't hear you."

Not that he would hear her even if he didn't sing, but maybe it would set her at ease.

"I'd rather you didn't." Her voice was louder now as another blast of wind cut across the flat valley bottom. "It might be more off-putting."

He chuckled at that. Humour. It was out of place, but it made him feel she was growing more comfortable around him now.

When he remained silent, she softly said, "Saint? Could you sing?"

He leaned his back to the wall, jammed his hands in his pockets and did as she had asked, singing an old country song she was sure to take the piss out of him over, pointing out how uncultured he was because he didn't know any modern tunes.

He hadn't made it far into the song before the door to his left opened. He stopped and looked at Holly, caught the awkward edge to her gaze as she lowered it to the snow and then lifted it again, meeting his.

"You have a nice singing voice."

That soft admission took him aback, had him standing there staring at her like an idiot. It was the first time someone had told him that.

Rather than trying to think of what to say in response, he muttered, "We should get back, before we both freeze."

She nodded and stepped down from the hut, closed the door behind her and started along the path ahead of him. He drifted along behind her, a strange sensation growing inside him, one that warmed him. Because she had admired his singing voice?

Pride swelled inside him, had him walking a little taller.

They were halfway to the cabin when a gust of wind came out of nowhere, making him almost lose his footing on the compacted snow.

Holly lost hers.

She slipped and her arms flailed, a shriek ripping from her as she started to go down. Saint lunged for her, grabbed her arm before she hit the deck and kept her on her feet. Barely. He pulled her up and she stumbled into him, slid again and braced her hand against his chest. Her grey-green eyes darted to his.

Hunger rolled through him, had him close to growling as his gaze fell to her lips, as a need to kiss her crashed over him. He stared at her mouth, wanted to groan as her lips parted in response, as his heart pounded a frantic beat against his ribs—against her palm.

The temptation to kiss her was great, but before he could muster the courage to bend his head and capture her lips, he noticed how badly she was trembling.

"You shaking because of the cold or because you're scared of me?" he husked, praying to the gods it was the former, even when he didn't like the thought of her being cold. It was better than the thought that she feared him.

Holly eased closer to him, openly seeking his warmth in a way that made him want to growl. "I'm freezing."

It was strange but addictive to have her this close to him, pressed up against him, even if she was only trying to steal his heat. He dialled back his need, caged his urges, and placed his arm around her. He tucked her against him, waiting for the inevitable protest.

She said nothing, just nestled closer to him, sinking into his side as they walked. Her steps were too slow for his liking, her breathing too shaky. He faced her, bent his knees, and scooped her up into his arms. She didn't even protest then. She sighed and snuggled up to him, her breath warm on his neck.

Gods, it felt good to hold her like this.

To take care of her.

It felt right.

He carried her the rest of the way to his cabin, didn't set her down until he had reached the couch. He placed her on it and looked her over, frowned at how pink her fingers were and her face. She didn't make him stop when he removed her boots, or when he rubbed her toes through her socks to get some warmth into them. She didn't even push him away when he removed her damp coat, revealing a basic red long-sleeved T-shirt that wasn't at all suitable for the weather conditions.

No wonder she was cold.

He rose to his feet and went to the door, closed it and hung her coat up and then stripped his off. He kicked his boots off and went back to her as she tried to lean forwards, stretching her hands out towards the fire.

Saint crossed the span of fur between her and it, grabbed the end of the couch nearest her and pulled it towards the log burner, moving her closer to it.

He cast a glance at her as she looked at him, gratitude in her eyes.

He sank to his knees in front of her again and rubbed her arms, quickly at first but the strokes slowed as he grew aware of her watching him, her eyes on his face. He lifted his to meet them, stilled as he lost himself in the look she was giving him, one that made him want to kiss her.

She had accepted his warmth. Would she accept his kiss?

Saint didn't think so, and he didn't want to frighten her, so he forced himself to stand again and went to the kitchen. He filled the kettle with water from a container he kept beside the sink and set it on the stove, and then hunted through the cupboards, looking for the packets of hot chocolate he was sure he had seen somewhere.

He wanted to growl when they eluded him, when he began to worry he would have to disappoint her and make her coffee instead. It wouldn't do. Her eyes had lit up when he had offered hot chocolate. He wanted to come good on his offer, wanted to see warmth in her eyes like that again when he presented her with the drink. If he had to go back out into the storm to find some in the larder, he would do it.

He breathed a sigh of relief when he moved a packet of pasta aside and spotted the hot chocolate sachets, grabbed them just as the kettle whistled.

Saint glanced at Holly from time to time as he prepared the drink for her, and one for him. She looked brighter now, the deep flush of cold gone from her skin, and it was a relief to see it. He picked up both drinks and carried them to her, set his down on the small table at the end of the couch and held hers out to her. She was quick to take it, to hug it in both hands, tucking it close to her chest as if it were precious and drawing a deep breath of the steam.

She sighed, the sound holding a hint of bliss.

Apparently, she liked hot chocolate. He made a mental note of that and then shook his head, because once the storm had cleared, he had to do the right thing.

He had to give her back to the cougars.

He stomped away from her as the thought of doing that soured his mood, ignored the heat of her gaze on his back as he walked to the cupboards at the far end of the room. He picked through his shirts, trying to find one that wouldn't swamp her frame. She needed something warmer to wear, something that wasn't as revealing as the figure-hugging T-shirt she wore. He wasn't sure how long he would be able to resist the urge to touch her again if he left her in just that flimsy garment.

He needed to cover her up.

Not too much though.

Just enough to shut down that urge that kept coming over him, one that was growing fiercer every time he felt it, that was slowly transforming into a need that was new to him—a desire to bend her to his will.

He fished out a blue checked shirt, sniffed it to make sure it was clean enough for her, and then carried it over to her. When he held it out to her, she scowled at it.

"I'm not wearing that." She sipped her hot chocolate, not taking her eyes off the fleece shirt, as if it might leap and attack her if she didn't watch it closely.

"Why not? You'll be cold in what you're wearing, and you can't wear your coat all the time. You'll be too warm." He held it closer to her.

She recoiled and glared at it, and then tipped her head back and hit him with a hard look. "You just want me to smell like you and I don't want that."

Saint arched an eyebrow at her. It hadn't been his intent, but good gods, he found it appealing. He was tempted to make her wear it now, wanted to stamp his scent all over her as Cobalt had, as Knox had, but reined it in, aware that if he pushed her, she would push back, and he was enjoying the calm between them.

He tossed it on the arm of the brown couch near her. If she got cold, it was there, an option she could choose to take. That primal part of him liked that idea even more. The thought of her choosing to wear something of his, intentionally rubbing his scent on her, had him on the verge of growling.

So he strode to the kitchen and busied himself again, grabbed the pasta from the cupboard and a pot, and focused on cooking it for her. He stared at the bubbling pot of pasta, deeply aware that she was probably going to find it basic too. If she mentioned his offering of pasta and sauce was subpar, he wouldn't take offence. Getting her to eat something was more important than avoiding another hit to his pride.

He strained the pasta and divided it onto two blue plates, added sauce from the other pan to both of them and then grabbed two forks and carried them to Holly. She was quick to take the plate from him, and even quicker to tuck into the food.

Not one complaint left her lips as she devoured it, and he enjoyed the comfortable silence as they both ate. When she was done, he took the plate from her and set it on his, and placed them both on the floor.

He sat back and stared at the fire. It would be good for a while, had enough logs to keep it going. He tried not to be hyper-aware of Holly where she sat beside him, close to him, but it was impossible. Her scent of berries teased him, her warmth made him hotter than the fire did, and nerves trickled through his veins, had him glancing sideways at her to see if she was as on edge as he was.

"That was nice," Holly murmured, no trace of nerves or fear in her voice. "Thank you."

He glanced at her, lingered as he found her looking at him, as their eyes locked for a moment before hers darted away, settling on the log burner. Maybe she was as nervous as he was about sitting together like this. It seemed crazy to him. It wasn't as if anything was going to happen, but he couldn't shake his nerves, couldn't stop his palms from dampening or his heart from racing.

Gods, he felt like a kid again.

Scared witless by a female, by the feelings she stirred in him, and the thought she might reject him if he dared to act on his impulses.

Holly tucked her legs up beside her and leaned back into the couch, and he sat with her, listening to the fire popping and the wind rattling the panes, debating what he was going to do. He wasn't talking about whether or not to kiss her either. This was bigger than that, something that had been on his mind from the moment he had realised she wasn't Ember.

Actually, it had been on his mind from the moment he had cooled down and realised what he had done. Kidnapping really wasn't his style. He blamed his bear side, blamed the cougars too for riling him when he was tired. Blamed himself. He should have had more control over himself. Should never have resorted to stealing one of the cougars as revenge.

It hadn't been his finest moment.

And it was unbefitting of an alpha.

He chuckled low as he thought about how reckless he had been back before he had been alpha. That part of him clearly hadn't changed. Sometimes, he still did stupid things.

"What's so funny?" Holly sounded sleepy.

He glanced at her, met her gaze again and saw in her eyes that she was tired, that everything was catching up with her now. He wanted to set her at ease so she would sleep, and maybe he could do that by opening up to her a little. Besides, he wanted her to know more about him.

"Thinking about when I took over the pride. I was… not really cut out for it."

Her dark eyebrows pinched and then relaxed. "Did you lose your parents?"

"Yeah, but they weren't the pride alphas. They were killed by hunters shortly after I matured." He sank a little deeper into the couch. "I'm the last of my line. Was raised here and lived here long enough to see it go from a good, happy pride to one that feared its leader."

She shuffled to face him, her grey-green eyes serious. "And you decided to do something about that."

He shrugged, but it came off stiff. "I couldn't let it continue. Saw too many good folks getting hurt... living their lives in fear. Like I said, I was pretty reckless back then. Guess I still am. Always leaping before I look... letting my bear instincts take the reins too easily."

He waited for her to pick him up on the fact he had kidnapped her, only she didn't. She just stared at him, her expression soft, firelight flickering over the right side of her face and bringing out the cougar gold in her eyes.

"I took the position of alpha through combat. Woke up one day in a bad mood and just walked right up to the bastard and challenged him. Caused quite a stir."

The corners of her mouth twitched slightly. "I can imagine. You seem to have a habit of doing that."

"I'm trying to get better. I try to do the right thing." He scrubbed the back of his neck. "Sometimes I screw up though."

She didn't look angry at him because of his screw up this time. In fact, the more time he spent with her, the more comfortable she looked around him.

"How long have you been alpha?" She looked at the fire again, her gaze lingering on it.

"Not sure. Four... five decades maybe." He studied her profile, wanting to gauge her reaction to that, sure she would piece together his age from the information he had given her.

If she did, it didn't shock or disgust her, because she continued to gaze at the fire, her eyes growing hooded. Maybe she was too tired to care about his age.

She had told him that she had matured. How recently? Long ago enough to have participated in the spring mating that took place at Cougar Creek every few years?

Hell, the thought of her taking part in it, inviting suitors to fight for the right to her, made him want to roar and kill every male in that pride.

He gripped the back of his neck instead, pressed his claws in and focused on the pain, shutting down his urge to lash out. She wasn't his. He had no claim to her. He doubted he ever would, and he deserved that lonely fate for what he had done to her.

Was there any way he could right his wrongs with her?

The war inside him reignited as two paths stared him in the face, one that was tempting and one that made him want to growl and rage.

Taking her back was the right thing to do.

But that meant letting her go.

"I think I'm secretly a bear too," she murmured.

He frowned at her. "What makes you say that?"

She yawned. "All this snow is making me sleepy."

Her little smile hit him hard, damn near punched a hole in his chest and seized his heart.

She sank against the back of the couch, resting her left arm along the top of it, and her head on that arm. "Tell me about the winter sleep. Cougars don't sleep through winter."

"Not all bears do." He relaxed a little further as he thought about what to tell her. "A couple of the bears in the pride don't. They head to the city for winter, enjoy the bars and restaurants, and the benefits that civilisation has to offer."

"You never do that?" She blinked at him, her eyelids heavy, and then opened her eyes wide and sat up a little straighter.

Trying not to fall asleep on him.

He wanted to tease her and ask if he was so boring that he put her to sleep, but didn't have the courage. "It's not my style. I need to be here to protect the territory and those who choose to stay here, and I prefer to sleep the winter away. Sometimes I'll stay awake longer, but once the snow sets in, the furthest I've made it is a few weeks before I succumb to the urge to sleep. As soon as Knox and Lowe are sleeping, it rolls up on me pretty fast."

"You don't miss being awake?" A small frown formed a wrinkle between her fine eyebrows. "I think I'd miss being awake. If you fall asleep when the snow sets in, how long are you usually sleeping for?"

He chose to answer her second question. "I sleep maybe... early November through to late May most years. Sometimes longer."

"Gods, that's what... six months? That's half the year!" She looked horrified by that, pulled a face that was almost a pout. "I can't imagine sleeping for six months. You must miss out on so much."

He grunted and gestured to the window. "Yeah, I'm missing a lot by sleeping through this kind of weather."

She leaned to her right, towards the log burner, her black hair swaying away from her slender shoulders as she peered past him. "I suppose you're right. It does make me sleepy. There's been so much snow that I've spent most of my time at the Creek curled up in front of the fire with a book."

"A book?" Colour him intrigued. "What kind of book?"

"Well. Books. Multiple. Many, many books. I have them on my phone."

He arched an eyebrow at her. "On your phone?"

She smiled and looked as if she might laugh, so he frowned at her, showing her he wouldn't like it.

"You can get books on your phone now." She sagged into the back of the couch on a long sigh. "I think I've read five... maybe six... since I arrived."

"What kind of books do you like?" He was enjoying this, how relaxed she was around him and how she was telling him more about herself. "Any you can recommend?"

"If you like romance novels." She looked him over. "You could probably pick up some pointers from them."

She clammed up, turned awkward as she averted her gaze, and he knew why. She feared he was going to pick her up on the fact she thought he needed pointers when it came to being romantic, and that meant she had been thinking about him in a romantic fashion. It was the only reason she could have for bringing up that he wasn't acting that way or at least he wasn't living up to the standards she expected from a romantic hero based on what she had read in books.

"How long were you sleeping before we woke you?" Her voice dropped to a murmur and she glanced at him, the look in her eyes telling him she felt bad about the fact her pride had woken his.

"About a month I think."

"And you just go to bed one night and wake up in spring?" Her eyes searched his.

"Pretty much."

"Does sleeping affect you physically? Like do you wake up weaker, skinnier?" A blush stained her cheeks.

His too as her gaze dropped to his body and she slowly raked it over him, a leisurely once-over that set his blood on fire.

He cleared his throat. "Not really. Takes a while to shake off the sleepiness and get my muscles working again, but it doesn't weaken me and I don't tend to lose much weight."

"And you could stay awake if you wanted?" She turned awkward again. "Dumb question. You're awake right now."

Gods, was he.

No danger of him nodding off when she was near him.

She looked close to falling asleep on him again though. She blinked rapidly, as if that was going to keep her awake.

"Saint?"

"Hmm?" He drifted in watching her as she tried to fend off sleep, enjoying how close to him she was and that she trusted him enough to let her guard down like this, and how calm he felt—both the bear and the man in him. She opened her mouth and closed it again, glanced away from him, and he sighed. "Whatever is on your mind, you can ask it, Holly."

Her brow furrowed. "When you grabbed Gabi—"

"I was in a foul mood and not thinking straight," he interjected. "Archangel had been flying around Black Ridge, had attacked Cougar Creek, and then this human female is there just days after it all happened. What was I meant to make of her? I was on edge, feeling protective of my pride, and things got out of hand. I'm not proud of what I did, or what I said. As soon as I cooled off, I... I should have apologised. I still think she's a hunter though."

"She isn't. Her half-brother was. She didn't know anything about his involvement with Archangel, was shocked to find out about it and about our kind."

He shrugged. "I'll apologise to her just as soon as Rath apologises for waking us and Flint apologises for attempting to remove my balls."

Her sigh said it all, but it didn't stop her from muttering, "Testosterone runs a little strong in bears, doesn't it?"

He frowned at her and grunted, not bothering to deny that. He was territorial, and protective, and his bear was quick to anger and take control, and there was nothing he could do about that. He was the way the gods had made him.

But maybe he could try to change for the better.

If he did, would she want him?

He glared at the fire, seeking the answer there as the war erupted inside him again. Taking her back was the right thing to do, but he feared that if he did, he would never see her again.

She made the decision all the harder as she dozed off, as she slumped against his right arm and snuggled into it.

When he tried to move, sure she would be horrified and angry with him if she woke pressed against him, she unleashed a low, vicious growl.

A possessive and commanding snarl.

One he felt all the way to his soul.

She seized his arm and he could only sit there, stunned as she rubbed her face against his muscles.

As if she was marking him.

He was one hundred and ten percent certain no one had ever scent marked him before. He had no right to enjoy it as much as he found he did, knew he should stop her but couldn't bring himself to do it as a thought formed.

Maybe he wasn't the only one feeling something.

Saint made his decision as he gazed at her, as she continued rubbing her cheek to his shoulder, a low rumbling growl like a purr rolling from her.

When she woke, he was going to ask her how she felt about him. And he was going to tell her how he felt about her.

CHAPTER 11

The sound of male voices roused Holly from sleep. She frowned, her nose wrinkling with it, and snuggled back down into her bed, drawing the covers up over her head.

"Just a few more minutes, Morrison," she mumbled, wriggled to get more comfortable and drifted off again.

This time, it was a roar that woke her, had her jerking upright and the fog of sleep dissipating, making her hyper-aware of her surroundings. She wasn't in her bed at home, and those voices hadn't been her brothers come to annoy her until she woke up.

Her heart started at a pace and she threw the blanket that had been placed over her aside, the feel of it irritating her now, making her feel as if she was being hindered as her instincts fired off a warning. Something was happening outside.

She shot from the couch as a series of feral, threatening growls answered the vicious roar, and shifted to face the open door of the cabin. A cold wind blew in, sweeping around her, but she didn't feel it as her blood burned, as her heart raced to pump it around her body and adrenaline surged.

Preparing for a fight.

Holly shoved her feet into her boots and raced to the door.

Her eyes widened and she rushed forwards as she spotted the huge grizzly bear facing off against three large cougars in the sunlit clearing in front of the cabin.

The brothers had found her.

Relief flooded her, happiness rolling in on the heels of it as she looked at the brothers, as she thought about returning to the Creek.

Those feelings were swift to die as Saint lurched forwards, huge right paw batting at the air, driving the three cougars back on the already trampled snow. The largest cougar, one she recognised as Rath, growled and bared fangs as he eased away from his brothers, moving to one side of Saint. The cougar she thought might be Storm because of the scar that ran over his flank moved in the opposite direction to Rath.

They were cornering Saint.

She shook her head and hurried onto the deck, cursed when she slipped in her haste to defuse the situation and fell on her backside. Pain rolled up her spine as her bottom hit the cold wood hard enough to rattle her brain in her skull.

Saint looked back at her, his brown eyes filled with worry she swore she could sense in him.

She gasped as Rath used the opening she had given him, pounced on Saint's back and sank his claws into his thick brown fur. Saint moaned and swayed, tried to bite Rath but he couldn't reach him as Rath manoeuvred himself, managing to get right onto Saint's back, his rear paws digging into Saint's lower half. Rath bit down again, growled as he only came away with a mouthful of fur.

Holly shook her head again as Saint reared onto his hind legs and dislodged Rath, growling the whole time, and Storm was quick to leap into the fray. Saint groaned and then roared as he brought his left paw down, aimed at Storm's head as he tried to nip at Saint's hip.

Storm was swift to leap back, but barely evaded Saint's blow. Saint's paw slammed into the churned-up snow, his snarl one of frustration now as Rath leaped on him again and he wasn't alone this time. Flint joined him, viciously bit at Saint's back, trying to pierce his thick hide.

Fear mounted inside her, panic rushing to tangle with it, and her hands shook as a fierce need rolled through her, fogged her mind and made it hard to think clearly.

She wanted to fight too.

Saint was stunningly savage as he reared again, as he swayed and threw Rath and swatted at Flint. Flint cried out as Saint raked claws down his flank, as he managed to throw him too. Storm launched at him, leaping high into the air, his front paws splayed.

He wasn't a match for Saint though. Saint batted at him, caught him hard in the midriff and slammed him into the ground, ripping a pained hiss from Storm. Before Saint could deal another crushing blow, Rath ploughed into his side, bit and clawed him, vicious as he defended his brother, buying Storm time to escape.

Holly was so caught up in the fight, her heart lodged in her throat as she battled the instincts roaring to life inside her, that she didn't notice someone sneaking up on her.

She shrieked as they grabbed her, reacted on instinct and clawed his arm, leaving long grooves in his black jacket.

"Shit," Cobalt muttered and scowled at her, his stony grey eyes filled with an unimpressed look as he caught her hand, stopping her from clawing him again. "Some greeting."

He grabbed her wrist and pulled her forwards, down the steps of the deck, and she stumbled along behind him, couldn't take her eyes off Saint as he fought the three cougars. She didn't feel the cold bite of the air through her red long-sleeved T-shirt as she watched him, felt numb all over.

Worry churned her stomach, had her heart beating faster and harder, as Saint took a bad blow to his face, Rath's claws leaving red grooves in his shorter fur. She pulled to a halt, forcing Cobalt to stop, her brow furrowing as the three cougars worked to take Saint down.

A feeling stirred inside her, a primal need that was strong and had her pulling Cobalt back the way they had come.

Towards Saint.

She had to help him.

He was strong, but it was three against one, and Rath, Flint and Storm were swift in their cougar forms, agile as they dodged Saint's attempts to even the odds.

Cobalt muttered things she didn't listen to as she dragged him forwards, resisting his attempts to pull her in the other direction, determination to reach Saint powering her, making it impossible for Cobalt to stop her.

She flinched as Saint batted Flint away, leaving himself open to Storm. Storm leaped on his back, viciously clawed at Saint's right shoulder, cleaving it open, and Saint loosed a mournful moan as he tried to shake Storm but couldn't. She didn't want to look as Storm sank his fangs into Saint's shoulder, yanked his head back and ripped a gash in it that spilled crimson.

The sight of all that blood tracking down his shoulder, soaking his rich brown fur, turned her stomach and a need surged through her.

A need to go to Saint and defend him.

Shock swept through her, that instinct stunning her enough that she forgot to fight Cobalt, couldn't muster the strength to resist him as he dragged her towards the trees.

She stared at Saint as she stumbled backwards, unable to take her eyes off him, off the way he was fighting.

Desperation. Rage. Fear. She swore she could feel all those emotions in him and could see them in his dark eyes as they leaped to her as he tried to throw Rath from his back, as he realised the distance between them was growing and he couldn't stop the cougars from taking her back.

Holly expected him to give up, to accept that he had lost and that she was no longer his captive.

He didn't.

He only fought harder.

He was vicious as he took on the three cougars, managed to land a few blows, but he wasn't fast enough. His size and his injuries slowed him down.

And his fear.

She could feel that emotion in him, could feel it growing as he wrestled with Rath and dislodged him, as he glanced at her again and took a hard hit from Flint.

Why fear?

Was he afraid of losing this fight?

A thought struck her.

Or was he afraid of losing her?

Flint smashed into Saint's head, colliding hard with him, and Saint went down, hitting the churned snow. His head slammed into it, his eyes glazed with pain.

She opened her mouth to call for him, an urge to break free of Cobalt's strong hold on her arm shooting through her, but stopped when Saint looked right at her.

Resignation shone in his eyes.

Resignation and pain.

She shook her head slightly as he tried to stand, willing him to give up, because if he didn't, the brothers would kill him.

Holly's brow furrowed as she stared at him, torn between going to him and leaving with the brothers so they would end their assault on him. Leaving won, because it was the only way to save Saint.

Her heart ached as she backed away from him, as he sank back onto the snow and stared at her and that fear she could feel in him grew, and she knew in her heart that it was fear of losing her.

"I'm leaving," she said, loud enough that all the brothers would hear her. "Leave the bear. He's learned his lesson."

When Flint and Storm looked as if they wouldn't halt their attack, only Rath moving to leave Saint alone, she realised she needed to give them a reason to end their fight. Flint and Storm were fighters, and both preferred to take on foes who were stronger than they were, challenging themselves.

Her only way of making them leave Saint alone was making him out to be someone unworthy of their time. Unchallenging.

She couldn't bring herself to look at Saint as she spoke, was aware this was going to hurt him, but it was the only way to help him.

"Look at him. It's clear he's no match for you. This is the third time you've beaten him. He's so weak even I could defeat him."

She turned away, guilt rolling through her as she felt Saint's gaze on her. She silently apologised to him, wished there was another way to make the cougars leave him alone, but this was the only one that had come to her. It was the only way that would work with Storm and Flint. Neither brother was going to want to fight someone that a female had openly declared she could beat. They had a little too much male pride.

As predicted, Storm and Flint broke away from Saint, padding towards her through the flattened snow.

Holly trudged into the trees beside Cobalt, her heart heavy in her chest as Saint continued to stare after her, slowly filling with a need to turn back and go to him, to make sure he would be all right and to apologise to him.

Every step she took that increased the distance between them killed her.

But it was the only way of stopping the brothers from killing him.

If she had to endure pain a thousand times worse than this to save Saint, she would do it.

Because she had the feeling she was falling for him.

CHAPTER 12

Saint wasn't sure how long he had been laying in the snow, still in his bear form. Staring at the trees. Staring after her.

Her words echoed in his ears. Cut him to the bone. Carved up his heart.

Her absence destroyed him.

He wasn't sure when he had given up on everything.

No. He was. Wasn't sure he would ever forget it either. It had been the moment she had walked out of his life without looking back. He had given up then, because without her, life wasn't worth living.

Voices wobbled around him and scents other than his own blood filled his nostrils, but he just remained where he was, staring after a female who didn't want him, who thought him weak, who hated him.

A female he wanted to call for, desperate for her to return. A female he needed more than anything. More than air. A female he felt sure had taken his heart with her when she had left him, leaving him hollow inside.

Dead.

"Oh my God. Don't go near that bear!" A female voice he didn't recognise rang out behind him, her scent unmistakably human.

A hunter?

Saint didn't care.

She could kill him if she wanted.

Although, death was coming for him anyway. His bones were like ice. His mind sluggish. Every rasping breath he managed smelled like blood.

His blood. It pooled around him, a huge patch of crimson that grew larger every hour, one that should have concerned him.

Only he couldn't muster the strength to care.

He just kept staring in the direction Holly had gone.

Aching for her to return.

"Shit, he looks bad." Lowe.

Black boots appeared to his left, red slush on their toes.

"I need to move him."

"It's a bear. You need to back away. I don't know what attacked him but—" The female voice cut off in a muffled, pained grunt.

Lowe huffed. "Let's get you to my cabin. All nice and toasty like. I'll deal with him, and then I'll deal with those fucking cougars."

"You can't shoot cougars! Regulations state…" Her words drifted into the distance.

Saint just kept staring at the trees, willing Holly to come back to him. She wouldn't. He knew that. She was gone, and he would never see her again. She had made that clear.

She had made her decision.

He moaned, the sound mournful, couldn't hold it back as that ache in his chest worsened, as the longing to see her again grew stronger. Killing him.

His vision tunnelled and everything went black for a second.

"Come on, now. No time to sleep." Lowe again.

The male sucked in a sharp breath as he eased to a crouch on Saint's right. Saint growled when the male reached for the wound on his shoulder, weakly baring his fangs at him.

Lowe edged his hand back, his voice unusually stern. "Fine. I'll give you a pass for now. But you need to move. Got it?"

Saint grunted and kept staring at the trees.

Lowe huffed and stood. "Don't make this easy on me or anything. When I hurt you, remember it's your own damned fault."

The male moved around him, and then walked away, and Saint lost track of him. Another black wave rolled over him and then receded as someone jostled him. He growled as his backside was suddenly lifted off the ground and lowered again, and he felt the bite of a rope around his hips. He started sliding backwards, that rope digging in uncomfortably, tugging another growl from him.

"At least the snow makes some things easier," Lowe grunted, his voice strained as he hauled Saint somewhere.

He didn't care where.

When his rear half lifted higher and his chin smacked off something hard—a wooden step—he snarled and grunted, decided he did care. He tried to wriggle free of Lowe's grip, but didn't have the strength.

Could only watch as he was pulled further from the forest. Further from Holly.

Towards somewhere warm.

Lowe stopped hauling him and muttered behind him, shifting things around, and then came back to him.

"Getting your fat ass into this cabin is going to hurt. Just remember… it's your own damned fault." Lowe grabbed the rope and began tugging.

Saint growled and groaned as the bastard attempted to squeeze his backside into the doorframe, as he felt as if he was being crushed. He pushed onto his back feet, tried to shuffle forwards, only he didn't have the strength to escape Lowe and return to gazing at the forest, and ended up flat on his stomach.

"Thought that would get you moving." Lowe sounded as if he had just scored a victory, when all he had done was invite a very painful death.

Saint would deliver it once he had a little of his strength back. He just needed to sleep for a while. Maybe forever. He sagged, slumping against the floor, darkness beckoning again.

Lowe gripped his hind legs, pulling them out behind him, and shook them.

"Don't sleep now, buddy. Rise and shine."

Saint moaned at him, the low rumbling groan sounding sorrowful to his ears. Defeated.

"What's gotten you so down, anyway? So the cougars took the female back. You should have known it would happen." Lowe hauled him backwards into the cabin.

Saint dug his front claws into the wood, splintering it as he tried to anchor himself and stop Lowe from pulling him away from that female.

A female he had known would leave him eventually.

He had wanted to talk to her before that happened though, had been sure that if he had told her that he was starting to feel something for her that she would admit she felt something for him too.

Only she didn't.

She had made that painfully clear.

He gave up fighting as warmth curled around him, thawing his numbed legs. Two instincts warred inside him, one the desire to survive at any cost that had been roused by the warm kiss of the fire on his fur, and the other a powerful need to give up because life without Holly would be an empty existence.

Lowe pulled him in front of the fire and Saint just lay there, his front and hind legs stretched out on the floor.

"You look like a fucking rug." Lowe moved around him and went to a cupboard near the stairs, grabbed a large black bag and came to him.

He set it down near Saint's head and ignored him when Saint bared fangs at him, warning him away.

"Yeah, I'm about to let you bleed out. I don't think so." Lowe pulled bottles and bandages from the bag and scowled at him. "You could make this a lot easier on both of us by shifting back."

Saint didn't think he could. In this form, the hurt was easier to deal with. His bear side didn't do complicated. Emotions were dulled while he was embracing that part of himself. If he was hurting this badly in his bear form, he didn't want to think about how much pain he would be in if he shifted back.

It would kill him.

So he was resolved to stay a bear, had decided it would be that way until he died from blood loss and exposure, but now it would be until all the feelings for Holly that had been growing inside him withered and died.

However long that took.

Probably forever.

Saint wasn't sure he was ever getting over her.

Because he was sure she was something to him, something special. Something once in a lifetime.

His fated female.

A fated female who didn't want him.

He wouldn't be the first male whose true mate had rejected him, but that didn't make it hurt any less. It went no way towards dampening the pain that was ripping his heart to shreds.

Lowe tended to his wound, muttering things, holding a one-sided conversation that Saint tuned out as he stared through the open door, across the field of churned and bloodstained snow, to the woods that separated him from Holly.

The urge to go to her was strong, had him restless with a need to stand. He shut it down. She didn't want him. Going to her would only end in him being hurt worse. Yet he couldn't convince that need to die, found himself biding his time, slowly pulling himself together, thanks to that ridiculous tiny seed of hope. He tried to stand and Lowe shoved him back down.

"Now you get feisty?" Lowe huffed and went back to tending to his wounds. "Just lay there and accept your fate."

Saint wasn't sure he could. The larger part of him wanted to do just that, was resolved that his life was over now that Holly had left him, but that tiny seed of hope was already growing, spreading tendrils through him, whispering words about fighting and winning her back.

Winning her heart.

Would she give it to him if he did things right this time?

His bear side grew restless too, his instincts growing stronger as his body warmed, as he stopped losing blood. They filled him with a dark need to go to the female, to make her come with him, and to fight anyone who tried to stop him.

Because she was his.

He growled when someone dressed in black obscured his view, jogging up the steps to his deck to draw to an abrupt halt in the doorway.

"Christ! What happened to him?" Knox stepped into the room and sank to his knees beside Lowe on the wooden floorboards.

Lowe flinched in time with Saint as he dabbed at the wound on Saint's right shoulder, cleaning it. "I came back and found him out in the snow like this. Don't know how long he was out there, but I do know it was the cougars. The female is gone. Place reeks of them."

"I'll murder them." Knox's voice lost its sharp edge as he looked back over his shoulder, into the clearing. "Gods, look at all that blood. You think it's all his?"

Lowe nodded, his expression grim and blue eyes saying the opposite to his mouth. "He'll be fine."

The bear didn't believe that, and the look on Knox's face said he didn't either.

"I was about to kick your ass for running off like that, but now... I'll save it for later." Knox ran a shaky hand over his dark blond hair, mussing it. "I don't want to think about what would have happened if you hadn't come back here. Someone needs to put those cougars down."

Lowe slid a look at his brother. "No one is going off to start a war. Saint needs us here."

"Why didn't he just shift back and come inside?" Knox eyed the wound and then his twin. "Wound like that is painful, sure, but no reason to lay out in the snow waiting for help."

This time, Lowe's silent look conveyed the answer to that question—Saint hadn't been waiting for help.

He had been waiting for Holly to come back.

Or death to take him.

Saint didn't make a fuss as Knox stood and moved to his rear and worked to warm him up, massaging his stiff legs and drying his fur with a towel. He didn't make a fuss whenever Lowe hurt him.

He just kept staring at the door, at those woods, thinking about Holly and how she had cuddled up to him, had scent marked him and growled when he had tried to stop her, and had looked at him as if she had wanted to kiss him.

He thought about how she had looked at him out there in the cold and what she had said. The two seemed to contradict each other. Her words had been harsh, meant to wound, to hurt him. Her eyes had shown fear for him, worry and a fire that had told him she had wanted to fight.

And it hadn't been him she had wanted to attack.

It grew darker outside as he replayed everything on repeat, as his bones finally stopped aching and his muscles no longer felt like liquid beneath his skin, and the pain of his wounds fell away. He tried to keep still for Lowe as he worked, taking care of his smaller injuries now, but he was restless as he watched night fall.

As the need to see Holly grew stronger, close to overwhelming him, a driving force that compelled him to go to her and tell her everything, before he lost her forever.

But the need to sleep was stronger still as warmth soaked into him, as everything caught up with him, as he felt safe with his kin nearby to protect him. To watch over him.

He fought to remain conscious, fearing that if he slept now, he would be sleeping for some time, that a healing sleep would become a winter sleep and he wouldn't wake until spring.

Until it was too late.

Holly would leave Cougar Creek soon and he knew in his heart she would never return.

Darkness overpowered him, dragged him down into it, and he battled it with all his strength, even when he knew he couldn't stop it from taking him. As he sank into it, one thought echoed in his mind.

Would he wake in time?

Or would he never see Holly again?

CHAPTER 13

Worried didn't cover how Holly felt as she sat on the red couch in Ember's lodge, not really paying attention to anyone as they crowded around her. All she could think about was how much blood there had been.

How pained Saint had looked.

How fiercely she ached inside.

"I told you we should have put the bastard down when we had the chance," Storm growled, long strides chewing up the distance between the wall to Holly's left and the kitchen to her right as he paced in front of the fireplace.

She curled her fingers into fists, saw Saint all over again, covered in blood, moaning in pain.

"Did he hurt you, Holly?" Rath eased down to crouch before her, his grey eyes holding a wealth of concern. Blood tracked down his cheek from a cut there, and it wasn't the only one he had.

When Storm, Rath and Flint had shifted back and dressed in clothing they had stashed in the woods, she had seen all the wounds Saint had given them, and it had turned her stomach. She had expected to feel a sense of guilt, or perhaps remorse, because they had been hurt too and she had thought only of Saint, but that feeling hadn't hit her.

She felt sure she should feel terrible about what had happened to Rath and his brothers, and should feel grateful to them for rescuing her and bringing her home to the Creek.

But she didn't.

She only felt bad about what had happened to Saint.

She only wanted to see him again.

"Look at her. She's in shock. Gods only know what that brute did to her." Flint snarled those words, ignoring his beautiful black-haired mate as she tended to a particularly nasty gash on his upper left arm, just below the sleeve of his navy T-shirt. His grey eyes flashed fire as he shoved his dirty fingers through his short onyx hair, and bared short fangs as he growled. "Storm's right. We should finish him off once and for all. Look at what he did to Gabi."

Gabi who had remained with Ivy in Rath's cabin, the two females waiting there for their mates to return.

"Don't get me started." Storm paced harder behind her, the aggression that rolled off him stoking Holly's own.

Making her want to lash out at everyone.

Fight everyone.

"Storm," Rath said, his voice calm and even but firm enough to convey a silent order to his younger brother, a demand that he dial it back. His warm grey eyes dropped to Holly again and he placed his left hand on her knee. "You can talk to us, Holly. What happened?"

"I think we can all guess what happened. He tried to take Gabi, Rath, and he was pretty damned clear about what he had wanted to do with her," Storm bit out.

Holly shot to her feet, almost knocking Rath on his ass, and startling everyone in the room. They all stared at her, expressions blank.

"I need some air," she muttered and turned towards the door, but Rath was on his feet before she could move a step, had his hand wrapped around her arm.

"You stay. I think we're the ones who need some air." Rath gave her a tight smile and then looked at Storm and Flint, and Yasmin. "Let's give her some space."

They all filed out of the lodge, but they didn't go quietly. Storm and Flint held a terse conversation as they walked, painting a horrible picture of bear shifters, and a fire blazed to life inside her again, filling her with a need to go after them and correct them, to argue with them about everything they believed.

Because they were wrong.

Saint had been savage and quick to rage, but he had been gentle with her too, had shown her kindness at times, a glimpse beyond the veil to the man behind the bear. They were wrong about him where Gabi was concerned too, and she wanted to chase after them and tell them everything Saint had told her, wanted to explain what had happened and why Saint had threatened the female. They wouldn't believe her though. They were hellbent on hating him.

And in a way, she couldn't blame them. He had given them every reason to think badly of him.

Holly slumped back onto the seat of the red couch, all of her fight leaving her, because no matter what she said to her friends, they would never change their opinion of Saint or his kin.

"Did he hurt you?" Ember sank to her knees before her, her pretty face soft with concern, her black hair tied in a knot at the back of her head, revealing the mark on her nape.

A mark Saint had checked her for.

When he had seen no such mark on her nape, she had sensed the relief in him, and a wicked heat had curled through her as he had stared at it.

Was he all right?

She looked off to her right, at the window. It was getting dark now.

"Answer the question," Cobalt growled and Holly glared at him. He instantly backed down, the hard edge to his expression softening as he eased down to sit on the coffee table. "Sorry. I'm not trying to be a dick. We're all just worried about you, Holly. We just want to help you. We all know how cruel bears can be. They've been nothing but trouble since we moved into the area."

Something inside Holly snapped.

"They've been nothing but trouble?" She frowned at Cobalt, refusing to back down when his grey eyes narrowed on her, cougar gold emerging in his irises as his fair eyebrows pinched hard. "You know we could have avoided all this if we had just been good neighbours and offered to keep the noise down?"

Cobalt blanched, his face going slack. "What do you mean?"

"Saint took me because he was angry. Rath refused to keep the noise down and his pride couldn't sleep. Apparently winter sleep is very important to bears. He asked Rath, only wanted to help his pride, and Rath said no or something." She didn't have the full details, wished she did now because Cobalt was starting to look more than shocked.

He looked guilty.

It hit her.

"You told Rath to refuse him. Who else convinced Rath to be an asshole to Saint?" Holly stood again, couldn't remain sitting as the fire inside her blazed hotter still, stoked to an inferno by the thought that Cobalt had been responsible for what had happened to her. "I knew Rath wouldn't have been so inconsiderate."

Cobalt squared up to her. "He got what was coming to him, Holly. He tried to kidnap Gabi. He almost killed Flint."

"I'll admit, one of those was unprovoked, but Saint was on edge because of the recent fight with the hunters and Gabi is human, so he thought she was a hunter... and I don't think I need to remind anyone that Flint picked that fight." Her blood was boiling now, and while part of her was bone-deep aware that standing up to Cobalt like this was a recipe for disaster, the rest of her couldn't back down. "And you picked this fight with him when you told Rath to refuse Saint. Rath should have known better. He's lived here long enough to know that Saint's blood runs a little hot and his bear side is quick to come to the fore when he's angry about something. We all have moments where our instincts seize control and we do something stupid. Bears are no different."

"Saint." Cobalt looked down at her, towering a good foot taller than her, just as Saint did.

Only when Saint tried to intimidate her like this, she didn't feel afraid of him.

"You keep using his name, Holly," Cobalt drawled, a calculating edge to his grey eyes as that shimmer of gold in them brightened. "You best friends with the bear who abducted you now?"

"No," she bit out, maybe a little too quickly judging by how Ember's eyes widened slightly. She shook her head. "I'm not... but he didn't hurt me. Okay? He didn't lay a finger on me. As soon as he cooled down, he realised his mistake. He was sorry about it. He's sorry about everything he's done wrong and maybe if you gave him the chance, he would apologise about it."

"Oh, so he was the perfect gentleman?" Cobalt arched a blond eyebrow at her, ignoring Ember as she wrapped her hands around his arm, clutching it through his black cable-knit sweater, trying to make him back down. "He kidnapped you. He took you hostage to upset us all."

Holly kept her mouth shut when words bubbled up, ones about the fact Saint hadn't really meant to take her. He had wanted to take Ember. Telling Cobalt that would only push him off the rails.

"Cobalt." There was black magic in Ember's whisper, a spell that seemed to blunt the edge of Cobalt's mood as he looked at his mate.

He sighed and backed off a step, and then another, giving Holly space.

When he was in line with Ember, he turned and raised his hands, framed her face and murmured throatily, "I just keep thinking about... What if he had taken you?"

Holly was relieved she hadn't mentioned that had been Saint's plan now.

Cobalt dipped his head and captured Ember's lips, his kiss sweet at first, but as Ember tiptoed and pressed her hands to his chest, it turned passionate.

Feeling that the two of them weren't going to stop anytime soon, Holly backed towards the door, surrendering to her growing need to be alone with her thoughts.

Ember cracked her eyes open and looked at her as she kissed Cobalt, worry in her gaze.

Holly shook her head and smiled. "I'm really tired. Just want to be alone for a bit."

Ember looked as if she might try to convince her to stay in the cabin, but Cobalt growled against her mouth and pulled her closer, banding his arms around her curvy waist. Distracting her friend.

Holly hurried from the cabin, grimaced as the cold hit her. She rubbed her arms through her long-sleeved T-shirt, trying to keep the chill off them as she strode through the woods, her heightened vision making the path as clear as day to her. She didn't slow until she reached Cobalt's small territory. The snow had piled up in the clearing, but the storm had swept it away from the front of the raised L-shaped cabin.

She waded through the snow, legs growing colder and stiffer by the second. It was slow going, sapped her strength as she kept her gaze locked on the front of the cabin, her thoughts on getting inside and warmed up.

And being alone.

She had never needed to be alone more than she did at that moment.

Her feet were numb by the time she reached the steps. She kicked the snow off each wooden board, working her way up to the deck. When she reached it, she glanced out at the clearing and paused to take in how beautiful it was with the snow glittering in the slender moonlight and the stars sparkling above the mountains.

Only for some reason, it wasn't as beautiful as it had been when she had admired the view before.

She looked off to her left, up the valley.

Towards Black Ridge.

A need to keep on walking, to go back to that place, flooded her but she forced herself to go inside instead. The air was chilly inside the cabin. She kicked snow off her boots and removed them, winced as her feet touched the icy floorboards and hurried to the fireplace on the right of the open-plan room.

She busied herself with making a fire, letting her mind empty as her hands went to work, purging everything the brothers had said about Saint and his kin, and how tense she had been when they had been crowding around her. Cobalt was bound to report everything she had said to Rath, and she only hoped it might go some way towards making her alpha see that Saint wasn't a bad bear. He just had a bad tendency to let the bear in him take the reins when he was angry and made poor decisions while his more animal side was in control.

She slowly relaxed by degrees, and by the time she had lit the kindling and the first flame caught and began to spread, she was beginning to feel at ease again.

Holly pushed to her feet and wriggled her toes as they steadily warmed, stared at the flames dancing across the logs and lost herself a little in them. In the silence. It was bliss.

She pulled down a deep breath.

Smelled cedar and snow, and wanted to growl. She lifted the left side of her T-shirt, pressed the material to her nose and breathed deep of that earthy scent. Her eyes slipped shut, calm flowing through her to chase the chill from her skin and the ache from her heart.

Saint.

Tears lined her eyelashes as she saw him fighting, as she saw him take a bad hit and watched crimson roll down his side.

Holly opened her eyes, not wanting to relive that moment, and hurried from the fire, heading for the sleek, modern kitchen. She opened the cupboards, looking for hot chocolate.

And found Cobalt's whiskey.

Well, it would certainly warm her up.

She grabbed it instead and a glass from another cupboard, and carried them to the grey couch that faced the fireplace. She sank into it, uncorked the bottle and poured herself a glass. Sniffed it and grimaced as her nose stung. She had never been one for drinking, but she had never been one for a lot of things before.

Like feeling attracted to someone.

Wanting someone.

Holly shuffled into a more comfortable position on the couch and tucked her feet beside her. She stared at the fire as she nursed the glass of whiskey, sipping it, and then sighed as she clutched it to her chest. Her thoughts turned to Saint again. She was sure she should be glad to be home with her pride, but she missed the brute.

She worried about him.

For the first time in her life, she had found a male who had awoken feelings in her, needs that had been strong.

Were still strong.

She mulled over everything the brothers had said about him, trying to see in him what they did and weighing it against what she knew herself.

What she felt.

Was she like those people who fell for their captors, because they had grown accustomed to them and had been shown glimmers of kindness by them?

Saint had been kind to her at times, but she hadn't exactly been held by him long enough to grow accustomed to him at all or view him through rose-tinted glasses. He had his rough edges, could be savage just as the brothers had painted him.

Holly sipped the whiskey again, enjoying the burn.

Thought about her time with Saint.

Right back to when he had grabbed her in the woods.

She could have escaped him then if she had shifted. Some part of her was deeply aware of that. Why hadn't she? She frowned as she remembered why. She hadn't wanted to shift. Something about Saint had made her not want to fight him.

Something about him had made her feel other things too.

Wicked things.

And things that had been frightening at the time.

Like an uncontrollable need to dominate him.

And a powerful desire to protect him.

That need had been unmistakable when the brothers had attacked him, when she had seen him desperately fighting them and had felt sure he had been afraid of losing her. A need had run through her.

A need to shift and defend him.

Holly poured another glass of whiskey and thought about how the brothers acted around their females. How Ember acted around Cobalt.

She swallowed it in one gulp as something dawned on her.

There was one reason she might be feeling possessive and protective of Saint.

The big gruff bear might be her fated mate.
Holly set the glass down and stood.
She needed to know for sure.

CHAPTER 14

Holly left at daybreak, refreshed from a night of fitful sleep and slightly worse for wear from a few too many whiskeys. The coffee she had downed had done nothing to wake her up, had only made her more jittery, so on edge that she hadn't been able to eat anything.

It had been a fight to convince herself to wait for dawn before heading to Black Ridge, a trial that had taken its toll on her, had allowed horrific images of Saint bleeding out to sear themselves on her mind and fear to make a home for itself in her heart. There was no purging it now, not without seeing him.

She glanced off to her right as she hurried from the cabin, a war erupting inside her. She didn't have time to talk to the brothers, and knew in her heart that if she did try to speak with them things wouldn't go the way she wanted. They wouldn't understand. They were hellbent on hating Saint and his kin, would only try to persuade her to remain at the Creek.

Worse, there was a chance they would stop her.

Holly tugged her purple woollen hat down and burrowed into her scarf as she hurried from the deck, her heart pounding at the thought of what she was about to do. Ember would be worried about her, and the brothers would probably be mad at her if they discovered she was gone, but she had to go.

She needed to know Saint was all right.

Needed to know if he was her fated mate.

She would be quick, would get to Black Ridge and back again before anyone realised she was gone.

The recent snowfall tried to make that impossible, was up to her thighs in front of Cobalt's cabin. Holly waded through it, forced to head down the clearing slightly to reach shallower snow and then bank left, towards the woods. The snow crunched beneath her boots as she sank into it with each step and chilled her legs through her black salopettes. She focused on reaching Saint, trying to ignore how cold she was already, keeping her eyes locked on her destination.

A breeze chased around her and she wrapped her arms around herself, trying to keep the chill off. Her dark green jumper offered some protection from the weather, but she began to miss her coat more and more with every stride she took across the open ground.

The towering pines and spruces offered shelter from the snow as she reached them, made it easier for her to walk as she wove through the sea of their broad trunks and even kept some of the chill from her skin as they provided protection against the wind.

The nerves she had been fighting since waking this morning began to break free of their tethers, rose again with each step that brought her closer to Black Ridge. The trek through the forest seemed to take forever, but she remained on the animal track, following it down into deep pits filled with twigs and bracken, and up the high rises on the other side. Her senses placed the river to her right and she tracked it around the sweeping bend that separated Cougar Creek from Black Ridge.

Just as she was beginning to feel that she had taken the wrong turn somewhere, voices cut through the still air.

She instantly recognised them.

"What's wrong with him?" Knox's voice rang clearly across the snow and she hurried to the edge of the woods and sheltered behind a tree so he wouldn't spot her. His black woollen hat had been pulled low over his blue eyes, but she easily recognised him as he stood at the bottom of the steps that led up to Saint's cabin.

While he and his brother looked the same, there was a cruel twist to Knox's lips, a darkness about him that Lowe didn't possess.

"I don't know." Lowe shoved fingers through his ash-blond hair as he stepped out onto the deck of Saint's cabin. He sighed. "It's like he's just given up or something. He shifted back last night and I want to take that as a good sign, but…"

That didn't sound good.

Her heart started at a pace again, the urge to break cover and hurry to Saint making her jerk forwards, past the shelter of the tree that had been her hiding spot.

Knox immediately whipped to face her.

Busted.

Rather than turning tail and running back to the Creek, she stepped out from the trees and marched through the snow, mustering her courage as she closed the distance between her and the twin bears. When she reached the spot where Saint had fought the cougars, she kept her gaze fixed on Lowe, didn't want to look at the crimson patch of snow where Saint had gone down.

Lowe dropped off the deck to join his brother, remained close on Knox's heels as he stormed towards her.

"What the hell do you want?" Knox growled, the aggression that rolled off him rousing her own, making her want to bare her fangs at him and show him that she wasn't going to be cowed by him.

She wasn't afraid of him.

"I think I left my coat." She shot for breezy with a dash of sarcasm. When she glanced at the cabin beyond them though, her bravado faltered. She reached out with her senses, seeking Saint, and fear swept through her. Fear for him. It sobered her, had her voice dropping and losing its bite as she focused on him. "I came to see Saint."

"Come to finish him off?" Knox moved into the path of her gaze and she did growl at him now.

"No," she bit out, anger blazing through her, quickening her blood as she faced him, as the need to fight that she had felt yesterday when Saint had been battling the cougars rose again, making her want to lash out at Knox and Lowe. "I just need to know if he's all right."

Lowe scowled at her and stepped aside, coming to stand beside his twin as he folded his arms across his chest, forming a wall with Knox. She growled again as she took a step forwards, aiming to go around him, and both males countered her, making it clear they weren't going to let her past.

She ignored Knox and looked at Lowe, sure he would be more reasonable than his twin. It took all of her will, but she wrestled the urge to fight into submission, calmed her instincts and gentled her tone, keeping the bite from it.

"Please. I just want to know he's okay."

Lowe's blue eyes softened slightly, a flicker of worry shining in them as his brow furrowed and he opened his mouth to speak.

Knox beat him to it. "The state of our alpha is none of your concern, cougar."

She looked between Lowe and Knox, and her heart grew heavier as she realised that convincing them to tell her how Saint was doing wasn't just going to be difficult—it was going to be impossible.

Knox had convinced Lowe not to help her the night Saint had taken her, and he was going to do all in his power to stop his brother from helping her now. She couldn't blame him. He was only doing his job as a member of the pride, protecting his alpha and keeping him safe.

"I know you're just trying to protect him," she whispered as fear and the need to see Saint got the better of her, merged within her to make her ache as it birthed despair that drowned out her anger, pushed her rage to the back of her mind and had hope leaching from her. "I just need to see him. If you won't let me see him, then at least tell me he's all right. I heard you. You said there's something wrong with him."

And her mind was running wild, conjuring images of him dying.

She couldn't take it.

Lowe's handsome face softened further. Knox's remained hard and unyielding.

Holly sighed.

Convincing them was going to take more than she really wanted to admit, but if it meant she got to see Saint and see that he was going to be all right, then she would put it out there.

"I swear, I don't want to hurt him." She looked them both in the eye, let her guard drop and let them see that she was telling the truth, and how miserable she was—how afraid she was for Saint. She thought about him, thought about her time with him and what he had said to her, and tried those words on for size, and they felt right. "I don't think I could hurt him."

She really didn't.

The thought of hurting Saint turned her stomach. The thought of him being hurt utterly destroyed her. She frowned as she realised something. She already had hurt him. When she had talked of his strength, when she had called him weak, she had only said those things to make the brothers leave him alone. She had done it to save Saint.

But it had hurt him.

She had seen it in his eyes.

"Bullshit," Knox snarled.

Lowe grabbed his arm when he went to step towards her, fire blazing in his blue eyes.

"Give her a chance." Lowe looked at his brother. "We're not getting through to Saint, but she might."

Worry twisted her stomach into knots again. "What's wrong with him?"

Knox gruffly shoved his hands into the pockets of his heavy black winter coat. "His wounds are healing but he refuses to wake."

"Maybe it's just the winter—"

Knox cut her off. "This isn't that. This is something else. Lowe thinks he's given up."

"Given up?" She looked at Lowe, those knots pulling tighter, making her queasy.

Because she had the feeling she was responsible for his condition.

Lowe nodded, his shoulders relaxing as he looked behind him at the cabin and then back at her. "I found him in the snow. I think he was there for hours. It was getting late by the time I came across him. I got him inside and patched him up. He shifted back and I thought maybe he would wake, but he won't."

Fear grew stronger inside her with each word he spoke, something crystallising as she replayed the fight between him and the cougars.

He hadn't given up when he had been fighting, had gone all out and not backed down, but the look that had filled his eyes when she had belittled him to stop the brothers from attacking him had been one of despair.

Of hopelessness.

Of pain.

Lowe was right and he had given up.

He had given up when she had left him.

Holly shoved past Knox and Lowe, ignored them as they growled and broke into a dead run, desperate to reach the cabin before they could stop her, her heart in her mouth and her mind on one thing.

Bringing Saint back to her.

CHAPTER 15

Saint was dreaming. Had to be. The light brush of fingers through his hair. The sweet smell of berries. It all had to be a dream. A torment. He was aching for Holly and here she was.

He could feel the heat of her pressed against his hip, the warmth of her flowing into him as he drifted in the darkness, easing the chill from his bones and thawing his blood. The delusion didn't end there. He could hear her voice too, swore she was saying his name in a hushed, gentle tone.

"Wake up, Saint."

He didn't want to obey that command, didn't want to wake. He just wanted to sleep forever, until this nightmare ended. Or maybe he wanted to hold on to this dream of her. Here he could have her. Here she wanted to be with him.

This place wasn't a dream.

It was Heaven.

Maybe he had died after all. Maybe this was the other side. A place where he could be with Holly just as he had wanted, could have the female he felt sure was his fated one. The only female he needed.

"Wake," she urged, her voice like summer sunshine.

He basked in it as her fingers danced down his cheek to brush his whiskers and then dropped lower to stroke his jaw, heat following in the wake of that tender caress.

Wherever she touched, he warmed.

And he felt loved.

This Holly loved him. He could feel it in that touch, and gods, it brought tears to his eyes, tore down his strength and humbled him because he didn't deserve it.

"Come back to me."

Now Saint knew he was dreaming.

She had wanted to be away from him, and he couldn't blame her, even when it hurt him. He had done everything wrong from the start. He had listened to his bear side too much, had been too tired to fight it, and by the time he had mustered the strength to be gentler towards her, it had been too late.

The damage had been done.

Hadn't it?

Her thumb brushed his lower lip, a tantalising caress that had tingles chasing in its wake.

"You're scaring me now," she murmured, her voice growing more distant as he relaxed into the darkness, her gentle touch easing the tension from his body and his soul, making him feel heavy again.

Bone-deep tired.

He wanted to apologise for scaring her too. He had frightened her. More than once. He had felt her fear when he had been fighting the cougars. She had been afraid for her kin, had been scared he was going to hurt them. He hadn't wanted to hurt them, but they had been trying to take her from him, and his instincts had gone wild.

"I wasn't afraid for them, Saint... I was afraid for you. I wanted you to stop fighting. You were hurt."

He frowned as she responded to his thoughts. Had he spoken them aloud? Perhaps it was because he was dreaming and, in this dream, she could hear his thoughts.

"I'm not a dream." Her voice was thick, laced with pain and uncertainty, with that trickle of fear he could sense in her.

Her hand lowered to his right shoulder.

"This looks bad."

She stroked fingers over a bandage there.

Warmth splashed onto his bare chest.

The scent of salt filled his nostrils, mingling with the berries.

Tears?

He had to be dreaming.

But he needed to be sure.

Saint cracked his eyes open, grimacing at how dry and sore they were. He blinked the grit away and frowned as his gaze sought Holly and found a hazy figure where he swore she was. He blinked harder, squinted to clear his vision.

Stilled as he found Holly sitting on her knees beside him, a beautiful look of concern etched on her face and her eyes filled with tears. A smile wobbled on her lips. Fleeting. Gone too soon. He ached with a need to cup her cheek, to comfort her, but he was so damned tired that he couldn't move, could only stare at her and hope she wasn't a figment of his imagination.

His beautiful Holly. His strong female. She hadn't cried when he had taken her from the Creek, hadn't cried when Knox had frightened her, hadn't cried when he had kept screwing things up with her, but now there were tears in her eyes. Tears for him. Born of fear.

She was crying for him.

Another first. No female had ever cried for him before. No female had ever looked at him like that either, as if she was on the verge of dying too, as if the sight of him hurt was killing her.

His eyes slipped shut again and he had to force them open, desperate to keep looking at her, sure she would disappear on him if he didn't. Sleep beckoned but he fought it, resisted the call of it as he stared at Holly.

Her grey-green eyes drifted down to his shoulder, turning solemn as her brow furrowed.

"I'll heal," he croaked, swallowed to clear his throat and added, "I'll heal quickly... now you're here."

He was sure of that as he walked his fingers over the furs towards hers, as he claimed her hand and she didn't tense. As she looked at him with soft, warm eyes. He pulled on her hand and she didn't resist him. She sank onto her side on top of the covers and rested her head on his bare chest as if it was the most natural thing in the world for her to do.

Hell, it felt as if it was.

He couldn't get over the fact that she was back with him—that she had come back to him. He had been sure he had lost her and would never see her again, but here she was.

"Are you really here?" he mumbled, afraid of the answer to that question, a small part of him still convinced he was hallucinating all of this and that any moment he would wake to find himself alone.

Or worse, would find Lowe standing sentinel over him, demanding he get better.

Her warm breath skated across his chest, teasing him. "I'm really here."

She placed her palm over his heart and the tension that had been building inside him instantly dissipated.

"That's good." He placed his hand on hers, curled his fingers around and clutched it.

That warmth she stirred in him flowed through every inch of him as he held her, making him feel at peace, as if everything was right in the world again and now he could rest. He could heal.

"I'm sorry I said those things." She tensed as she whispered that, stiffening against him, pulling him back up from the sleep that had been claiming him. Her head shifted against his chest, silken hair caressing his skin, and her gaze seared his face. "I just wanted them to stop hurting you. I didn't mean to hurt you too."

Saint pulled her a little closer, pressed his fingers into the soft wool of her jumper and held her a little tighter. The pain that had been a constant in his heart from the moment she had walked away from him finally eased, as if she had removed a thorn from it and kissed it better for him.

She reached up and feathered her fingers down his cheek. "Sleep. I'll be here when you wake."

He still tried to fight it, didn't want to risk it in case he woke and she had been a dream. He wanted to stay here in this moment with her forever, holding her like this, feeling at peace.

His body had other plans though.

Sleep overtook him, pulling him back to the darkness.

When he woke again, the instant fear that claimed him was quick to wash away as he felt the light weight on his chest, one that was pleasant and warm, and offered him comfort as her scent of berries drifted around him. He held Holly to his chest and sifted his fingers through the gentle waves of her black hair as he dozed off again.

Someone growled.

Not him.

Not a bear.

Cougars.

A fight erupted outside, luring him up from sleep, and stealing the female from his arms. Cold replaced the warmth of her and he did growl now as rage rolled through him, as every instinct fired and demanded he get her back in his arms, tucked safely against him. He fought the powerful grip of sleep, tried to shake it loose as he heard the door open, as snarls and growls reached his ears.

Knox. Lowe. He needed to protect them.

He needed to protect his female.

"Return Holly, and maybe I won't kill you." The familiar male voice belonged to Storm and Saint wanted to snarl as his fangs elongated, as fur rippled over his skin.

No one was taking Holly from him.

Sweet berries.

His heaven.

He couldn't lose her again.

Saint rolled and hit the floor with a grunt, pushed to his feet and stumbled as his head spun, the loft twirling with it, and his knees gave out. His head hit the mattress as he slumped onto it, his upper half resting on the furs while his bare knees pressed into the floorboards. He sucked down a deep breath.

Caught Holly's scent.

Holly.

He couldn't let them take her. He shook off the dizziness and mustered his strength, limited as it was, another thing that made him want to rage. He pushed up again, grabbed the jeans someone had slung over a chest and sank onto the edge of the bed. Almost lost his balance and rolled right off the damned thing.

He fumbled with the jeans, growing increasingly frustrated as he tried to get his feet into them. He was stronger than this. He was an alpha and his pride were in danger.

Holly was in danger.

On a low growl, he tackled his jeans with a renewed sense of purpose, managed to get his bare feet into them this time and tugged them up his legs. He stood and locked his knees as they wobbled, pulled his jeans up and snarled at the fiddly buttons, cursing them.

"Cameo, go back inside." Lowe hollered that order and followed it with a vicious growl. "Take your eyes off her, cougar."

Cameo? Saint vaguely recalled smelling a human female, hearing her talking to Lowe when he had found him in the snow. Lowe was keeping the female at Black Ridge. That tore a growl from him for a different reason. He would be having words with Lowe once he had driven the cougars away.

"You into kidnapping too?" Cobalt growled that question.

"Fuck off," Knox answered. "You don't know shit about my brother. You don't know anything about any of us."

Cobalt scoffed. "Know enough to know you'll get your asses kicked if you don't hand Holly over."

No. It wasn't going to happen. Not on Saint's watch. Holly had come back to him. She had chosen him. He wouldn't let the cougars take her again. He needed her.

He reached for the newel post at the top of the wooden spiral staircase, gripped it so hard he was sure it was going to crack under the pressure, using it to support himself. He shuffled forwards, fighting another dizzy spell as his right shoulder ached and every muscle in his body protested about being used.

Saint gritted his teeth as he shifted his left hand down to the railing mounted on the wall, as his leg almost gave out beneath him and he had to grab the banister with his right hand to stop himself from falling.

Pain blazed through his shoulder, an inferno that stole his breath and filled the air with the scent of blood. He glanced at the bandage, at the spots of fresh crimson seeping through the cream material, and clenched his jaw as he pushed onwards, unwilling to let the injury slow him down.

Nothing would stop him from protecting Holly.

He reached the bottom step and swayed left, grabbed the kitchen counter and used it as a crutch as his vision blurred. He squeezed his eyes shut and shook off the dizziness, dragged down a breath and forced himself to keep moving.

Saint mustered his strength, aware he would need it when he reached the door, when he stepped out onto the deck to deal with the cougars.

He had to protect Holly.

Had to stop the males from taking her.

He reached the door and gripped the frame hard, lifted his head to assess the situation and froze.

Stunned by the sight of Holly standing just in front of Knox and Lowe, facing off against the cougars.

Her own kin.

Defying them and defending him.

CHAPTER 16

Fired up didn't feel like a strong enough word to convey how Holly felt as she woke in Saint's arms and sensed Ember, her alpha and his brothers outside, when she heard Knox and Lowe telling them to back off.

And realised her kin had come for her again and were determined to steal her away from Saint.

It was more like someone unbolted the cage on a feral, primal part of her she had never known existed, freeing it and launching her into action.

She was powerless to resist that fierce part of her that roared at her to protect Saint, to stop the cougars from trying to hurt him again, and to drive them away and stop them from trying to take her from him.

Before she knew what she was doing, she was at the bottom of the stairs, blood thundering in her ears, skin tight with a need to shift and growl, to snap fangs at those who wanted to harm Saint.

"Holly," Rath said as she stopped in the doorway, as her gaze zipped from him to Cobalt where he stood to his left, and then to Flint and Storm where they flanked the two males, and finally Ember where she lingered behind them. "You're safe. We'll get you out of there soon."

Holly frowned at him. Get her out of there?

It struck her that they thought Saint had kidnapped her again.

Maybe she should have at least spared a few minutes to scrawl a note explaining where she was. She grimaced at that. It was too late for that sort of thinking now. She had to defuse the situation and make them see that they were wrong.

"Return Holly, and maybe I won't kill you." Storm stepped up beside Cobalt, his bright grey-gold eyes fixed on Knox. Storm wanted a fight—it was right there in his eyes as he narrowed them on Lowe, sizing him up.

Lowe looked off to his right.

"Cameo, go back inside," Lowe hollered and then unleashed a vicious growl when Holly looked in that direction too and spotted a female standing on the deck of his cabin. "Take your eyes off her, cougar."

At first, she thought he was talking to her, but as she turned to face him, she found Cobalt looking in that direction.

"You into kidnapping too?" Cobalt tossed Lowe a black look, one that promised pain.

"Fuck off," Knox snarled and closed ranks with his twin, flexing his fingers as he stared Cobalt down. "You don't know shit about my brother. You don't know anything about any of us."

"Know enough to know you'll get your asses kicked if you don't hand Holly over." Cobalt scoffed and folded his arms across his chest, and Holly didn't fail to notice that all of the brothers wore only dark jeans and T-shirts.

Everyone had come here prepared for another fight, had dressed in as little clothing as possible so it wouldn't hinder their shift if they needed to make one.

Lowe peeled off his black coat and tossed it aside.

Things were going to go south fast if she didn't do something.

"Saint didn't—" she started, but the males spoke over her, making her want to growl and attack all of them.

"Come on, Holly. They won't dare attack you." Flint held his hand out to her and rolled his fingers, his face etched with hard lines as he glared at Knox and Lowe. "If they do, I'll make them regret it."

"Yeah? I'd pay to see that. You only won against Saint because you clawed his balls, you sick fuck," Knox snarled and took a hard step forwards, his fingers curling into tight fists now. "How about I claw your balls and see how well you fight?"

Cobalt and Storm stepped forwards as one, Storm cracking his knuckles as hunger blazed in his brightening eyes and Cobalt running an assessing glance over Lowe.

They were going to fight.

Fight.

That word echoing in her mind had heat rolling through her, a fierce and powerful urge to shift chasing in its wake. She wanted to fight. She needed to fight. It was the only way. She felt that deep inside her, heard it roaring in every hard beat of her heart, compelling her to obey it.

If the cougars wanted a fight, she would give them one.

She was moving before she could stop herself, shoved a stunned Knox and Lowe aside as she pushed between them, and wiped the smug look off Storm's face as she growled and bared her fangs at him, threatening him rather than going to him for protection.

Daring him to try to take her or to try to reach Saint. She wouldn't let these males near him. She wouldn't let them disturb his rest. She wouldn't let them take her.

Because this was where she wanted to be.

She was done doing what she was told.

She was going to do what she wanted to do.

"I wasn't kidnapped." This time. "I came here by choice."

Neither Storm nor Flint looked like they believed her. Rath looked worried. About her? Cobalt was too busy staring down Knox.

Ember peeked her head out from behind her mate. "You did?"

Holly looked into her grey-blue eyes and nodded, drew down a breath and sighed it out as some of the tension flowed from her. "I needed to see he was all right."

"Why?" Storm bit out. "He was holding you captive, Holly. You shouldn't give two damns about him. You should want him dead."

She growled and flashed fangs at him, followed it up with a glare. "The last thing I want is Saint dead. You don't understand. None of you do."

"I'm thinking you don't understand." Flint glanced at Rath and spoke out of the corner of his mouth. "This some kind of Stockholm syndrome thing?"

Rath shook his head, a frown knitting his dark eyebrows and narrowing his grey eyes. "Let her talk."

She wanted to thank Rath for that, for being the only one other than Ember who was willing to listen to her, to actually take in what she was saying and trust she meant every word.

"Saint... He might have taken me hostage, but he was never rough with me." She looked to the blue sky, fighting for the right words, ones that would convince the brothers she was telling the truth.

"It doesn't change what he did." Storm levelled a black look on Lowe when he moved, and she was surprised when the bear stepped up beside her.

"Saint isn't a bad male—" Lowe started.

Storm cut him off with a scoff. "Yeah, tell that to my mate."

She could see things were heading south again, knew she had precious little time to convince her kin to back down and leave. That feeling intensified as Knox came to stand on the other side of her.

"I thought you were just a little overwrought yesterday when you argued with me, but now I'm starting to think the bears have brainwashed you." Cobalt looked her right in the eye, and she wanted to curse him as he added, "I figured you just needed some sleep and you'd forget this nonsense in the morning. See things right, like."

"Overwrought? Just needed sleep?" She hurled each word at Cobalt as anger built inside her, because he was treating her just as her family did, as if she was delicate because she was female and incapable of making her own decisions. "I'm not a child, Cobalt. What I feel for—"

She cut herself off, losing all momentum as she stared at the brothers, at Ember, feeling as shocked by what she had been about to say as they all looked.

Rath stepped forwards, concern washing across his face, softening his rugged features. His tone was gentle as he held her gaze.

"What do you feel, Holly?"

She clenched her fists beside her hips and wrestled with herself, trying to vanquish the part of her that said to keep her feelings to herself. She couldn't, because they were the only way to convince the brothers to leave

Saint alone and make them believe she was telling the truth and had come here to check on him.

"I feel…" She pulled down another steadying breath, gathered her courage and steeled her nerves as everyone looked at her, including Knox and Lowe. The weight of expectation was crushing, had her wanting to bolt and escape their gazes, but she pushed onwards. "Saint is my fated mate."

"Took you long enough to figure that out, Holly."

That deep baritone coming from behind her sent a shiver traipsing down her spine and had her spinning to face the owner of it as shock rolled through her.

Saint stood in the doorway of his cabin, leaning heavily on the frame, his dark eyes warmed by what looked a lot like affection to her.

Her heart lodged in her throat as she stared at him, unsure what to say, deeply aware that he knew what he was to her. She wanted to curse him, wanted to ask him why he hadn't told her, wanted to run into his arms.

Rath spoke before she could do any of those things, dragging everyone's attention to him, including hers.

"You're sure?" His deep voice was soft, laced with concern that shone in his grey eyes as he looked at her.

Holly swallowed hard and nodded, feeling lighter inside as she looked into his eyes and saw he believed her, and stronger for putting it out there.

"I felt as if I was going crazy when I was near him and that I would go crazy without him." She rubbed her arm through her green jumper. "I needed to get back to him."

"Sounds like what I went through." Ember stepped up to Cobalt and slipped her hand into his, linking their fingers as her mate gazed down at her, love in his eyes. Ember didn't take her gaze away from Holly. "Is there anything else you feel where Saint is concerned?"

The shimmer of heat in Ember's eyes told Holly exactly what she was talking about.

Holly zipped her lips and threw away the key, because there was no way she was answering that question in public. Her friend knew about her man problems. A problem she really didn't have with Saint. He had her firing on all cylinders. Just the feel of his gaze on her back was enough to have her blood heating and wicked thoughts filling her mind.

"You could have picked a better day to go running off after your mate," Storm grumbled and shifted foot-to-foot, agitation rolling off him that had nothing to do with a need to fight the bears.

Her eyes widened as the reason for his uneasiness hit her.

It was his wedding day.

She looked at Rath, feeling horrified as he smiled slightly at her and she noticed the strain in it.

It was their wedding day, and she was ruining it.

She covered her mouth with her hand, wasn't sure what to say as guilt flooded her, as she cursed herself.

"Oh gods," she whispered, her brow furrowing as she looked at both males, and then at the sky, charting the position of the sun. It was already getting late. "I'm sorry. I'm so sorry. I forgot… and I only meant to check on Saint and then come back to the Creek, but I fell asleep."

She looked at Saint. She didn't want to leave him, but she had to. She wanted to be there at the ceremony with the others, sharing this joyful moment with them. A joyful moment she hoped she hadn't ruined.

"Ivy and Gabi swore not to divorce us the moment we were married as long as we got you back to the Creek." Rath ran a hand around the back of his neck, his expression gaining an awkward edge. "So… want to do your alpha a favour and come back for now?"

She glanced back at Saint, loath to leave him. He was holding his shoulder, hand on the bandage wrapped around it, and she could tell he was fighting a grimace for her sake, didn't want her to feel bad about having to leave him again when he was in pain.

"Our neighbours could join us for this celebration," Rath said and Storm grumbled something under his breath.

"You rowdy bastards will only keep us awake anyway. We might as well attend." Saint's tone was gruff, drew a smile from her that became a frown when he pinned Rath with a hard look. "This truce lasts just the day."

Rath nodded.

Holly had the feeling that it was going to last a lot longer than that as Saint looked at her, heat and need in his eyes, hunger that echoed inside her too.

"I want to talk to you about what's happening between us," he said.

Panic swelled inside her, nerves quick to ignite. She needed a moment, was quick to take the out Rath offered her.

"Later. If I'm any later to my wedding, I might find myself without a mate. You have two hours, bears. Don't be late." Rath held his hand out to her and she hurried to him, walked past him and felt him turn to follow her, together with his brothers and Ember.

Holly glanced over her shoulder at Saint.

Already aching to see him again.

CHAPTER 17

Saint was nervous as hell. Not just because he was going to a damned wedding for cougars of all things, but because he was going to see Holly again. It felt as if he was the one getting hitched as he dug out his best clothes and brushed them down, and neatened his appearance. Gods, he hoped she wasn't too let down by the sight of him. He didn't own fancy clothes suited to the occasion. The best he could do was black jeans, a plain black dress shirt, and his heavy snow boots.

He scrubbed his face again, stared in the mirror on the wall near the stairs of his cabin and debated trimming his beard.

Knox opened the door. "Ready?"

Saint wasn't sure he was. That one word was enough to have his nerves rising, growing stronger, as he reached for the buttons of his shirt. His shoulder burned, ached as he wrestled with the first one, and he gritted his teeth.

"Here." Knox crossed the room to him, swept his hands away and took over buttoning his shirt for him. The bear muttered, "Still not sure why I have to go. Lowe got a pass."

Lowe had been given a *pass* as Knox put it because of the problem in his cabin. It turned out that Cameo was a parks ranger in serious trouble, and Lowe was extremely territorial about her.

Had almost run Saint off when he had gone to speak with him.

"It'll look better if it isn't just me," Saint growled.

"And you need a wingman." Knox finished with the last button and grinned at him. "Admit it. You don't want to face a pride of cougars alone."

Saint refused to admit that, even though it was the truth. He did want Knox there so he had some company, and some backup in case things didn't go well. He was fully expecting a frosty reception from most of the cougars, and knew from experience that it was going to take a lot for Rath to keep the peace.

"There's bound to be good food and plenty of alcohol at the party." Saint strode towards the door and grabbed his thick winter coat, flinching only a little as he pulled it on and zipped it up.

Knox perked up. "Bribery might get you everywhere."

The bear rubbed his stomach through his own black jacket.

Knox squeezed past him and opened the door, held it for him and closed it when he had passed. Saint took each step down to the ground with care, not wanting to slip and ruin the only passable clothes he had. When he hit the snow, he trudged across it, focusing on the thought of seeing Holly again and talking to her to shake another bout of nerves.

The cold made his shoulder ache, souring his mood as he walked in silence with Knox through the woods, following the track to Cougar Creek. He glanced at the male, caught the worry in his blue eyes before Knox masked it with a smile. He wasn't worried about the celebration with the cougars. He was worried about his twin.

"We'll make sure nothing happens to him." Saint lifted his left hand and placed it on his shoulder, squeezed it tightly through his jacket. "Even if it's the human female we need to protect him from."

Saint doubted Lowe would ever forgive them if they were forced to deal with her, but it was better than allowing Lowe to get hurt.

Voices came from ahead of him, pushing thoughts of Lowe and Cameo from his head. The nerves he had forgotten while thinking about his kin rushed back in and he exhaled hard, his breath fogging in the air.

"You sure she's the one?" Knox said.

Saint didn't hesitate to nod. "She's my fated female."

He smiled tightly at his friend. Maybe a little nervously judging by the amused glimmer in Knox's eyes and the way he patted Saint on the back.

"You'll be fine, big guy. Just… I'd say be yourself, but…" Knox grinned as Saint scowled at him.

His steps slowed as he spotted a white marquee ahead of them, one that had been set up in the clearing he had seen the cougars making in the snow. Warm white lights hung in sweeping lines around the top of it, illuminating the sides, and torches had been set around the grass outside it. Those torches led the way to a firepit too, circled it and the logs someone had placed around it.

Knox growled and Saint knew why.

Near the firepit, a huge grill was already on, the smell of meat flowing from it to make Saint's mouth water, and a table beside it had various dishes laid out and covered, just waiting for the post-ceremony celebrations. On the ground near it, there were two huge buckets filled with beers and wine on ice.

A few of the cougars milling around outside the marquee gave him and Knox funny looks, and he placed his hand on Knox's arm when he sensed the male's mood faltering, turning dark again.

"Let's go in." He jerked his chin towards the opening in the white tent, where ribbons of lights hung down to the floor on either side.

A long red carpet had been laid out inside, with wooden boards covering the grass on either side of it.

They reached the opening in the marquee and Saint drew up short as he almost ran straight into Flint. The black-haired male gave him an awkward smile and glanced inside the tent.

"Damned guys who were meant to be bringing the chairs couldn't make it." Flint didn't look happy about that as he looked down at a clipboard in his hand. "Everyone is going to have to stand. We're lucky half the guests made it after that little snowstorm kicked in."

Saint was beginning to wish none of them had been able to make it through the snow. He didn't like the way they all looked at him, as if he didn't belong there. There was no need for them to try to make him feel that way. He knew he didn't.

Saint shrugged it off, fought a grimace as his shoulder ached, hiding it from the cougar.

Flint looked as if he was going to leave without another word, and then he rocked back on his heels, that awkward edge to his grey eyes growing. "Sorry about the low blow I dealt you. I was courting Yasmin and had to do something dramatic to win her and... well... I shouldn't have done that."

Saint came dangerously close to growling at the male, because he didn't need a reminder of being laid low for a week because of this cougar, waiting for his balls to heal. The only thing that stopped him was the fact he had admitted he had been trying to win his female. His mate. Saint thought about what he would do in order to win Holly's love, and found there was nothing he wouldn't do.

Saint lifted his hand and Flint tensed, flinched away a little, and then relaxed as Saint merely slapped him on the shoulder rather than punching him as he had clearly expected. "Apology accepted. Not going to hold it against you. No bad blood between us, cougar... just... don't come picking fights at Black Ridge again."

"Thanks, man." Flint gave him a tight smile and hurried off, heading for the group of cougars. "Come on. Inside."

Saint caught Knox's arm and dragged him into the tent, ignored the gazes of the curious cougars who all looked their way and found a quiet spot near the entrance, away from all of them. Knox sighed and Saint knew why. The spot he had chosen was close to one of the patio heaters and the warmth of it was delicious, like standing outside in the summer sunshine.

Whoever had decorated the marquee had done a nice job of it. Strings of warm white lights had been draped between the walls and the high peak in the centre of the ceiling, and a cream painted trellis arch at the far end had the same lights woven among holly, mistletoe and ivy. All very seasonal.

He didn't need to tiptoe to see the faces of everyone in the tent, searched them all in a hunt for Holly, only he couldn't see her anywhere. Where was she?

Rath and Storm entered, both males dressed in black tuxedos, and Cobalt trailed in behind them, wearing a dark blue suit that hugged his broad frame.

Everyone hurried to greet the two grooms, and Rath and Storm smiled at everyone. The alpha even took a moment to look for him, smiled and nodded at the same time as Saint when their eyes locked. He wanted to ask Rath where Holly was as an uneasy feeling grew inside him, a fear she had been taken ill or something had happened to her, but he didn't get the chance.

Both males reached the arch where Cobalt had settled himself and was flipping through cards he held in a white-knuckle grip, radiating more nerves than the two grooms combined. Flint started the music and the crowd murmured, but Saint was too busy staring at the arch to pay attention to what was happening, his gaze fixed on the holly on it.

He needed to see his Holly.

Saint turned to leave as that need became too great to deny, stopped dead as she stepped into the marquee, a small bundle of white flowers held tucked to her chest in both hands.

Gods, she was breathtaking. Radiant.

A long, dark green satin dress hugged her curves, inflamed him and made him forget where he was. Made him forget his own damned name.

Cobalt growled low, a possessive snarl that echoed inside Saint too. Beside Holly, Ember blushed and cast a self-conscious look at her own deep green dress. They almost looked like twins as they walked as one down the aisle, with their raven hair twisted into a knot at the back of their heads and their grey eyes bright with happiness.

But one thing set them apart.

Ember had a mating mark on her nape.

His heart thudded hard when Holly shyly glanced his way before facing forwards again, and his gaze caught on her nape, on that patch of unmarked skin. He couldn't tear his eyes away from it, was sure she would be aware of him staring at it, aware of the hungers raging through him, a need that had him firmly back on edge.

He wanted to be the one to mark her nape.

He wanted to be her mate.

The two brides entered, Ivy wearing an elegant corseted white gown while Gabi had gone for a more conservative modern dress. He tried to focus on them as they approached their respective grooms, tried to pay attention to the ceremony, but Holly stole the whole of his focus.

He needed her.

And he would have her.

CHAPTER 18

The nerves Holly had managed to wrangle under control returned full force as she caught sight of herself in the mirror again. She wasn't sure she could do this, and she wasn't just talking about being a bridesmaid. The thought of seeing Saint had her restless, a little scared, and the thought of him seeing her in this dress had her wanting to run a mile. It revealed *everything*.

How had she not noticed that before?

The sweeping neckline plunged low, the loose folds of material that hung in front of her breasts baring a hint of cleavage, and the dark green satin hugged her hips and really showed off her backside.

Her fingers twitched at her sides as she stared at herself, as panic mounted inside her.

Ember placed her hands on Holly's bare arms, pressing against her back as she peered over her shoulder, looking at her reflection too. "You look killer, Holly. Saint is done for."

Holly hoped that was true. Ember had been telling her that from the moment she had put on the dress and had turned to Ember and sworn it was tighter than before, and far more revealing than she remembered.

"Come on. Let's go knock them dead." Ember looped her arm around Holly's and pulled her away from the mirror, led her to the cabin door where Ivy and Gabi were waiting, checking each other over for what had to be the millionth time.

Holly had pulled Gabi aside when she had entered, had relayed to her what Saint had told her about the day he had tried to snatch her, not wanting her to be on edge around him or afraid. Gabi had reassured her that she wasn't afraid of Saint and that she didn't hold it against him, mostly because Storm did that enough for both of them. Holly had a plan to get them together later in an attempt to smooth things over between them and hoped Saint would apologise for his actions.

Saint. Was he here? Her nerves returned as she thought about the fact he might be out there, waiting for her to make an appearance.

"Someone is miles away," Ivy's soft voice stole into her thoughts.

Holly shook herself back to the room and smiled an apology at her.

Ivy looked beautiful in her more traditional corseted strapless dress, her dark hair twisted in a plait at the back of her head, exposing her mating mark. Her hazel eyes twinkled as she helped Gabi fasten her short, white fur-trimmed cape over her shoulders and smoothed it down against her long, figure-hugging modern ivory dress that almost resembled the green one Holly was wearing.

Only Gabi's one had a slit up the left thigh that Holly was glad hers was missing. She was self-conscious in it enough without flashing her thigh with every step.

Gabi nervously checked her blonde hair, smoothing the braid that encircled her head like a crown, a flicker of fear in her blue-grey eyes. "I know we're already mated to them, but this makes it all feel horribly real."

Ivy laughed at that. "I wonder if they're feeling the same way?"

"Cobalt looked ready to pass out when he left us. If he's nervous, I can only imagine how Rath and Storm feel." Ember smiled and released Holly, picked up the two larger bouquets of white roses spotted with glittering diamante, and held them out to Ivy and Gabi. "Let's go find out, ladies."

Holly picked up her own smaller bouquet, thinking about what Ember had said. Was Saint feeling as nervous as she was? She wasn't really sure what to say to him when she saw him, and worried what he wanted to say to her. She hadn't imagined the first male to make her feel something would be the one male in the world for her—her fated mate.

Ember sighed and stroked her arm. "Come on. Quicker you see him again, the quicker you'll feel better. Just treat it like a date. You've had dates before."

"Yeah, but not with my fated one." And not with a male she wanted. She didn't need to say that for Ember to hear it, knew it as her friend gave her a sympathetic, warm smile. Holly blew out her breath. "What if I do something wrong? What if I make a fool of myself?"

By fool of herself, she meant hurling herself at Saint and climbing him like a tree in front of everyone to stake a claim on him.

When they had returned to the Creek, she had been faced with not only the brothers and their mates. She had been faced with half of her pride, and among the people who had made it to the Creek were close to a dozen unmated females.

All of them more beautiful than she was.

"What if Saint..." She couldn't bring herself to say it.

Ember pulled her into a hug. "Now you're talking crazy. I saw the way he looked at you, Holly. Saint is going to live up to his name. He's not going to be interested in anyone but you."

Gods, she hoped so, because she wasn't sure she would survive the blow if the one male she wanted ended up being more interested in someone else.

It was nerves talking. She was getting herself worked up over nothing, something which Ember had assured her was perfectly natural for a female when they found their true mate.

"If he so much as looks at another woman, we'll set the brothers on him... but not in a vicious brawl kind of way. I think he's had enough of that. I meant it in a make them corner him and teach him how a woman should be treated kind of way. Oh heck, screw getting the men involved. We'll do the cornering and teaching." Ivy beamed at her and Holly knew she was serious. "No man in this world can stand up to us ladies when we stick together."

It felt good to have Ivy, Gabi and Ember on her side. She had always wanted sisters, and Ember had grown to be like one for her, and now she had two more. She would swap her brothers for them in a heartbeat if she could have them as her real family.

She followed Ember out into the chilly afternoon air, breathed through her nerves as her gaze lifted to the marquee. Had Saint come? She hoped he had.

Flint anxiously shifted foot-to-foot outside the marquee, a look of relief crossing his face as he spotted the brides, Ember and Holly.

"About time," he muttered and looked them all over, flashing them a grin. "Ladies, you all look incredible. Let's get this show on the road. I need a beer. Someone brought their new baby with them and Yasmin is melting into a puddle over the chubby little bastard."

Holly tried not to smile, but Flint noticed her lips wobbling and frowned at her.

"I'd watch it… I swear Saint was looking fit to want one of his own just a second ago." Flint waved her away when her eyes widened. "I kid. I kid. I think maybe he wanted to eat it."

"Flint," Ember snapped.

Holly was too busy staring at the entrance of the marquee to chastise him herself, her heart drumming as awareness grew inside her, bringing her nerves back to the surface. Saint was in there. He had come.

And he was going to see her in this dress.

An urge to bolt shot through her.

Gabi pushed her forwards. "March your butt in there. Running solves nothing. Believe me."

Holly steeled herself and focused straight ahead of her, trying to shut out the rest of the world as the music started and she walked forwards. She felt Saint's eyes on her the second she entered, the feel of his intense gaze heating her blood to a thousand degrees and making her heart pound. She tried to keep her eyes off him, but couldn't.

One glance was all it took to suck the air from the room and electrify what remained.

Gods, he was handsome with his damp dark hair tousled and a black shirt hugging his broad chest.

His rich brown eyes seared her, sent another wave of electricity arcing through her, making her sizzle with awareness of him.

"Eyes front," Ember whispered out of the corner of her mouth, startling Holly into looking towards the altar. "You can feast on your handsome bear all you want later."

Holly wanted to growl at Ember for calling her bear handsome.

Her bear.

She shivered again as she felt his gaze on her nape, deep awareness rolling through her. He was her bear. He was hers and she was going to stake a claim on him. Her fangs itched at the thought, blood heating further as her mind raced forwards to imagine the moment.

She took Ivy's bouquet and drifted into position to one side of the altar, did her best to take in the ceremony and even teared up a little as the couples made their vows. She glanced towards Saint, wishing she could see him through the crowd. What did he make of this? It was unusual for shifters to have weddings, and she had never been to one before, but she loved it.

But not as much as she loved the shifter version of getting married.

A mating was a beautiful declaration of love and was an unbreakable vow. It was forever.

"You may now kiss the bride," Cobalt said, a look of relief flitting across his grey eyes as he lowered his cards to his side and his shoulders relaxed.

Rath gathered Ivy into his arms and kissed her, and Storm did the same with Gabi. Holly's heart swelled as she looked at the two couples, as she watched Ember going to Cobalt and kissing him too. She wanted the love that they all shared.

And she had the feeling she had found it.

She looked for Saint, grimaced as everyone crowded the two couples, pressing her towards them as they all hurried to congratulate their alpha and Storm. She pushed her palms against one male, twisted and reached for Ember, seeking a way out of the crush.

Her breath hitched as a gap between two people opened and she spotted Saint making a beeline for her, her lungs seizing as her gaze collided with his and she couldn't look away. Such hunger. Such ferocity. He pushed through the crowd, easily parting them despite his injured shoulder.

"Congratulations," he muttered to Rath and Storm, and seized her arm the moment he was within reach.

He pulled her through the crowd and over to one side.

"You all right?" His gruff tone backed up the spark of anger in his dark eyes. "You looked like you were getting squashed."

Holly shrugged it off, quivered from his touch as he flexed his fingers around her bare arm, the heat of his hand on it like a brand. She was on fire for this male, and he had to see it. His eyes dropped to her mouth, scalding her lips, rousing an ache.

A need.

She licked her lips.

Saint groaned and scrubbed his free hand down his mouth. "You look beautiful. You *are* beautiful."

She felt exposed as he gave her a slow once-over, his eyes darkening as his pupils dilated to devour the rich brown of his irises, the hunger that ignited in them unmistakable. Arousing. She shivered from his possessive gaze, had a hard time resisting the urge to throw herself at him after all.

Ember had been right. Saint was done for. She could see it in his eyes, in the need that sparked in them, one that wasn't all about desire.

"I want to get you away from all these males." His dark gaze flicked to beyond her, narrowed as it scanned the room.

His gaze strayed back to her lips and she knew what he wanted, because she wanted it too.

She didn't resist him when he led her to the entrance of the marquee where it was quiet and then out into the fading light, didn't feel the cold as she gazed up at him, unable to tear her eyes away from his lips or her thoughts away from finally kissing him.

She tensed, shaken from her reverie as his hands brushed her shoulders, and smiled as she realised what he had done. He gathered his coat closed around her and then drew her into his arms, trapping her hands against his hard chest. His heart thundered against her palms, rushing as fiercely as hers was as she stared up at his face, as anticipation swirled inside her and an ache formed, a desperate need only he could ease.

A flicker of a frown danced on his eyebrows, there and gone in a heartbeat, and then he dipped his head and captured her mouth.

Fire swept through her as he claimed her lips, his kiss possessive and fierce, dominant in a way that had her melting into him, on the verge of clawing at him as a need for more crashed over her. She leaned into the kiss, lost herself in it as his heat and his taste branded itself on her mind, as it roused a wicked urge to claw him anyway, to dominate him and stake a claim on him. She moaned and trembled, every inch of her quivering as he gathered her closer, as their tongues brushed and tangled.

She gasped at air, a little dizzy and wild with a hunger for more, as he pulled back on a curse.

"That was…" he mumbled, sounding unsure of himself, or perhaps he just felt as off-balance as she did as she swayed in his arms, hazy all over. "I hadn't expected that."

She tingled all over, aching for more as she murmured, "That was some first kiss."

He tensed.

Holly's eyes shot open, shock sweeping through her too, fear colliding with it.

"A first kiss for us… is what I meant. That was some first kiss for us." The words rushed from her, but she could see in his wide eyes that the truth was out there now.

He knew.

Her thoughts tangled and twisted into a blur as she stared at him, wanting to say something, to show him it wasn't a big deal, even when she knew it was.

"You can't miss the celebration." Ivy grabbed her arm, making her jump and blink, and throw a thank you to the gods as Ivy pulled her back into the tent. "You can play with the bear later."

Oh gods.

Holly glanced back at Saint, seared by the fire in his eyes.

She wanted that so badly.

CHAPTER 19

Saint was undone.

He couldn't move, could only stare after Holly as Ivy pulled her into the crowd, as his beautiful blushing female kept glancing his way, a flicker of nerves in her grey-green eyes. He couldn't think straight, could only repeat one thing in his head, over and over again, trying to make it sink in. Unable to believe it.

Holly was a virgin.

Untouched by any male.

A virgin.

Knox waggled a bottle of beer in his face. "You look like you need this."

Saint shook himself and grabbed the bottle, lifted it to his lips and drank it down in one go.

Beside him, Knox chuckled. "I admit, she does look stunning in that little number."

Saint growled at him, flashing fangs as an urge to rip his head off shot through him. Around them, several cougars fell silent and backed away. Knox held his hands up beside his head, his own bottle of beer dangling from the fingers of his right hand.

"Fair enough. I won't compliment her again." Knox was quick to back off a step when Saint growled again, just the thought of Knox looking at her enough to have him wanting to throttle the male, and then lash out at every unmated cougar in the area.

Knox went to the buckets and grabbed him another beer, looked at it and then grabbed a second. He came back to Saint and held both out to him.

"Not sure it'll help my mood," Saint grumbled but took the beers anyway, exchanging his empty one for them. He swigged the first one as Knox disposed of their empties and came back to him.

"You want to talk?" Knox shrugged when Saint growled low at him again. "Or not. We could just stand here drinking beer. Although, I'm feeling like the local freak a little."

Saint didn't like the way the cougars kept stopping to stare at them either.

"You think Lowe is all right?" Knox's tone gained a worried note as he stared into the tent. He took a long pull on his beer and sighed, his blue gaze shifting to his right, towards the Ridge. "Not sure what the deal is with this human."

Saint wasn't either, but he was determined to find out. "I'll talk to her tomorrow. I wanted to have a word with him before we came here, but your brother was… confrontational."

Something he usually left to Knox.

Knox took another long drink of his beer, his dark blond eyebrows meeting hard as he glared into the marquee. He was worried about Lowe, and so was Saint. Although he had the feeling he knew why the male had turned so territorial around the human.

It was the same reason he was feeling extremely territorial himself as Holly did the rounds in the marquee, smiling at everyone she spoke to, glancing at him from time to time. A virgin. He blew out his breath, sucked one down and held it as he tried to calm his bear instincts. Keeping them in check had been difficult enough before, but now it was impossible. Every instinct he possessed roared at him to go to her, to shield her from the gaze of every male, whether they were mated or unmated. A black need to lash out at them curled through him, had his hands tightening around the bottles he held.

They were suddenly gone, startling him back to Knox.

Knox frowned at him as he clutched his own beer and both of Saint's bottles. "You look ready to crush these, and I'm done doctoring your ass. I'll give them back if you swear you're not going to take out your aggression on perfectly innocent and good beer."

Saint huffed and snatched the one he had been drinking, lifted it to his lips and drained it. He sighed. "I can't help it. Look at her. She's beautiful... lights up that whole damned room."

Lit up his whole damned world.

Knox chuckled and shook his head. "Never thought I'd see you lovesick... and here we are. Got the feeling you're not the only lovesick bear at the Ridge either. Gods help me... I don't want to be next. Maybe Rune and Maverick can come back and throw themselves under the love-bus for me? Spare me the horror of settling down?"

Saint chuckled now. "The likelihood of either of them settling down is slim to none. I'm not sure they could handle a mate."

He sobered as he thought about that, went back to a night two decades ago, when he had raided the underground arena run by human hunters, one that catered to their twisted desires to watch shifters like Rune and Maverick trying to kill each other every night. Archangel were sick enough with their false noble cause to deal with only the dangerous non-humans, a lie used to cover the countless raids they carried out on peaceful shifters like his pride.

Like the one that had taken his parents from him.

Taken the parents of so many of his kind over the years.

The fact that there was also a faction within the hunter organisation that were running secret arenas made Saint want to return to his days of uncovering the locations of those disgusting places and taking part in raids on them.

Freeing the shifters they had forced to fight in the cages.

"You look ready to crush that bottle again." Knox didn't take it from him though. "Thinking about Rune and Mav?"

Saint nodded. "I'm worried about them. I know they both prefer to be in the city during winter, but..."

"I'll call Maverick. Let him know we're awake." Knox placed a gentle hand on Saint's left shoulder. "I'm sure they're fine. They always are."

Saint nodded, tried to make himself believe that. He always worried when the two of them left Black Ridge, fear that they would end up captured and put through that brutal torture at the hands of humans again lingering at the back of his mind.

"Watch your cougar. It'll take your mind off it." Knox tipped the neck of his beer towards the tent.

It would take his mind off it, but it wouldn't improve his mood. It took a sharp nosedive the instant he looked for her and found her dancing with Rath. The male was happily mated. He told himself that a thousand times as she smiled and talked to Rath. As he smiled at her and laughed. It didn't dull the edge of Saint's need to murder the male for touching what was his.

"I think I need a little air." Saint offered a tight smile to Knox when he looked as if he wanted to go with him, patted his shoulder and nodded.

Thankfully, Knox didn't follow him as he turned away from the marquee, heading for the bucket of beers. He set his third empty down in another bucket someone had placed beside the ones filled with beer and bottles of wine, and grabbed another beer. He carried it with him as he drifted past the grill and food, following the torchlit path to the firepit. The few cougars sitting there just glanced at him rather than stared, didn't stop talking.

Saint swigged his beer as he headed for the torches that formed a ring around the firepit, moved between two and stopped with them a few feet behind him. Before him, darkness stretched, but the moon was bright enough to cast highlights on the pristine snow that covered the rest of the wide clearing that reached down to the frozen river. It threaded the forest on the other side with silver and brightened the white caps of the mountains.

The murmur of conversation filled the silence, and he smiled as he heard Knox charming a group of female cougars. For a male determined not to settle down, he wasn't exactly avoiding female company.

Awareness of everyone fell away as Saint lifted his head and stared at the inky sky, watching faint aurora chasing across it. His breath misted in front of his face, the air growing colder as night closed in. He took a pull on his beer, savoured it this time, thought about how surrendering to the winter sleep meant he missed this sight. It was stunning. This far south, the aurora were weak, but with his heightened vision, he could see them clearly. He lost himself in their beautiful dance.

He tensed as a gentle hand came to rest between his shoulder blades, her palm searing him.

"It's cold," Holly murmured, her soft voice like music to his ears, seemingly making the aurora all the more beautiful. Or maybe it was the thought of sharing it with her that made it more bewitching. "Too cold to be out without a coat."

He slid a look at her as she stepped around him on his left side and groaned as he found her wearing his one again.

She smiled, her grey-green eyes sparkling with it. "Shame yours is taken."

Saint turned towards her, the aurora forgotten as she bewitched him instead. He moved his bottle and clutched the neck with two of his fingers against his palm, lifted his hands and tugged his coat closed over her. Held on to it as he gazed down at her, into her eyes.

"You took more than my coat," he murmured, warmth spilling through him, a trickle of nerves mingled in with it.

A blush darkened her cheeks and he lifted his left hand to cup her face and feel it.

His eyes leaped between hers as he thought about how they had come to be here, in this moment, and how grateful he was that it had happened. Grateful, but ashamed.

"I'm sorry for what I did... for everything." He smoothed his palm over her cheek, bathed in her soft look as she angled her head up, not a trace of anger or regret in her eyes. "I wish we'd met under better circumstances."

Holly sidled closer to him and pressed one hand to his chest, seared him with that touch, branding his heart with her name.

"Stop apologising." She brushed her fingers over his chest, idly stroking him. "I'll never be sorry that we met. I'll count my blessings every day."

Gods, she killed him. His beautiful, incredible Holly. A weaker female might have hated him, might have turned her back on him, but not Holly. She was strong on the inside too, was able to see past his mistakes and forgive him, to embrace the future without getting hung up on the past. He didn't deserve her.

He wanted to tell her that, but someone near the firepit muttered something about it being gone midnight.

Her gaze broke away from his, lifted to the stars that glittered above them, and she sighed.

"Christmas day." Her eyes dropped to his, a twinkle in them that made him want to know what she was thinking. "If I was home right now, my brothers would be throwing presents at me."

Her smile was stunning, hit him hard in the chest, knocking the wind from him.

"Brothers?" He frowned down at her, lifted his hand and tucked a rogue wave of black hair behind her ear, savouring the warmth of her skin beneath his fingers and how soft she was.

It hit him that there was so much he didn't know about her, so much they still needed to learn about each other, but he didn't feel panicked or unsure about what was happening between them, didn't begin questioning it at all.

Because there was one thing he knew for certain.

He wanted to spend the rest of his life with her.

They had all the time in the world to get to know each other.

And in his heart he knew that the more he learned about her, the deeper his love for her would grow.

She brushed her hair behind her ear again, her fingers briefly touching his, and shrugged, almost dislodging his coat. He drew it back over her shoulders, gathered her into his arms and held her as she battled the nerves he could feel in her. Nerves that ran through him too. They weren't about this conversation, or telling him about herself. They were about where they had left things the last time they had been like this.

She didn't need to worry. He wasn't going to make a fuss over what he had learned about her, and he wasn't going to rush her into anything. The ball was in her court. They had all the time in the world after all.

And every moment with her was precious.

"I have three brothers. All older... all obnoxious." She smiled and then grimaced, her tone shifting. "I don't mean that. I love them. They just drive me crazy. They always spoil this time of year when I love it so much."

"How do they spoil it?" Because Saint wanted to know how badly he needed to hurt her brothers to stop them from ruining a holiday that, while most shifters didn't celebrate it, clearly meant a lot to her.

She gave a little shrug and refused to look at him, dropping her eyes to his chest and her fingers as she circled one of the buttons of his shirt. Her voice was quiet when she finally spoke.

"They bring up how I managed to go another year alone."

Her pain flowed through him, and Saint decided that only death was a suitable punishment for how her brothers had treated her.

Because she was talking about them teasing her for not having a male.

Well, she had a male now. The one and only male she would ever have. And this male was going to make up for all the Christmas's her brothers had ruined for her.

"Do you like presents?" He liked it when she relaxed against him, when the tension he could sense in her faded, replaced with relief.

It struck him that she had expected him to growl and be angry with her brothers, or maybe tease her himself about how she had never been with a male.

While he wanted to do the former, there was no way in hell he would ever do the latter. He could never hurt her, and teasing her about the years she had passed alone *would* hurt her. He was hardly one to talk either. He couldn't remember the last time he had been with a female, felt sure it was long before Holly had matured. So long ago that as he thought about it, he started to get nervous too.

"I do love presents." She leaned into him, pressing her chest to his stomach and tipping her head back, gazing up at him with a little smile that said she didn't just love them—she *really* loved them. "It's not all about the presents though. It's the lights. The cold weather that makes you want to cuddle up indoors. It's being with those you love."

Her parents had named his fated female wisely.

He pressed closer to her, thoughts of cuddling up in the warmth with her chasing around his mind.

Together with being with the one he loved.

And he did love her.

"I could get you a present," he said, liking the way her eyes twinkled at him now, lit up as she half-smiled. "Although, I might not be able to get it right away."

She wrapped her arms around his waist. "There is something you could give me."

He stared at her, eager to know what it was.

Her gaze fell to his lips.

"A kiss."

CHAPTER 20

When Saint growled low, Holly was deeply aware that if he gave her this present, it wouldn't end there.

And part of her didn't want it to.

The rest of her was nervous, had been on edge from the moment she had accidentally revealed that her experience with males was a soul-crushing zero. She had tried to put it to the back of her mind when Ivy had pulled her into the marquee, had done her best to conquer her nerves as she had talked with the brothers and their females, and had even danced with Rath.

But the whole time, she had been aware of Saint's gaze on her. A need had steadily built inside her, a desire to go to him that had only increased whenever she had glanced his way and found females looking at him too. When the urge to bloody her claws had grown too powerful, she had even growled and bared fangs at one of them. Rath had chuckled and apologised for her, ever the alpha, and had ushered her towards the door, telling her to go to where her heart really wanted to be.

She had watched Saint walking away from Knox, drifting away from the crowds, heading towards the edge of the illuminated area of the sloping clearing, and had realised that deep in her heart, he was where she wanted to be. She wanted to be talking to him, snuggled close to him, bathing in his rare smiles and savouring the way he looked at her from time to time.

As if she was the only female in the world.

She wanted to feel the warmth of his skin under her palms.

Wanted to kiss him again.

Needed so much more than that.

"Holly," he husked and the slight tremble to her name gave away his nerves.

She reached up, took hold of his black shirt near the collar and tugged him down to her. He didn't hesitate to kiss her then, captured her mouth in a searing kiss that instantly inflamed her, had her heart racing and blood heating. She moaned, couldn't hold it back as his tongue stroked the seam of her lips and she opened for him, as he invaded her mouth and stripped away all her defences.

Saint's answering groan sent a thrill chasing through her, had her pressing closer, desperate for more, hungry to rip another low rumbling moan from him. She liked hearing his pleasure, loved how it stoked her own. She skimmed her hands up his neck, caught his nape, and deepened the kiss, growing bolder as his lips danced against hers, as he gathered her into his arms and pinned her against him.

The fire burning up her veins sparked hotter, an inferno that turned her reservations to ashes and unleashed her, freeing her of her inhibitions as it vanquished the nerves that had been plaguing her from the moment she had revealed she was untouched.

Holly tightened her grip on his nape, pressed her short claws in and growled against his mouth, the low feral snarl startling her a little as it pealed from her lips. She trembled as Saint growled back at her, as his fingers dug into her hips and she felt the command in that wicked snarl. The urge to dominate him rose swiftly, had her kissing him harder, attempting to push him into submission.

Saint didn't back down.

Electricity arced along her every nerve ending when he swept her up into his arms, tucking his left one beneath her backside and holding her on that side, away from his injured shoulder. She shivered as he gripped her nape with his right hand, as he seized control of the kiss.

Moaned as he started walking with her.

Her instincts fired, the most primal of them taking command, ripping control from her as she kissed and nipped at Saint's lips. She pushed his left shoulder, used some of her strength on him, feigning an attempt to break free of his grip, to escape him. He snarled against her mouth and held her tighter, crushing her against him, and she quivered at the feel of how strong he was. That display of strength tamed the wild part of her, had her purring as she kissed him.

She tangled her fingers in his dark hair and pulled his head back, savouring his growl of displeasure as she wrenched her mouth free of his. He frowned up at her, his dark eyes mesmerising her, holding her captive as she stared down at him. Holly wriggled against him, on fire for this male, fighting the instinct to push him harder, to make him lose control too.

When they reached the treeline, she dropped her head and claimed his mouth, swallowed his groan as she kissed him, teasing his tongue with hers.

A grunt burst from her lips as her back hit the trunk of a lodgepole pine. Saint grunted too, barely maintaining his footing, and then chuckled low as he breathed against her lips.

"Maybe we should stop kissing until we get to my cabin."

His cabin?

No. She wriggled, squirming in his arms, every instinct she possessed snarling at the thought of having to wait that long. It was too far.

She looked around them, realising that they had only just passed Ember's cabin. She wouldn't make it to Saint's home. She would explode before she reached it, felt too tight with need already.

He growled when she shoved his left shoulder, putting all her strength behind it this time, and twisted free of his grip. She grinned as her feet hit the ground, as she pirouetted away from him and evaded him as he reached for her. She lifted her green dress and began running.

For Cobalt's cabin.

The roar that cut through the still night air behind her sent a thousand chills skating over her skin, had her biting her lip as a fresh rush of arousal blasted through her. She breathed hard as she ran, her senses fixed behind her, that thrill growing stronger as she felt Saint chasing her.

And closing in.

Holly ducked around a tree, felt a little bad as Saint hit it and grunted, but thrilled too as he growled and kicked off, running harder. Chasing her. Gods, just the thought of him catching her had her close to the edge, on the verge of coming undone. She refused to slow though, obeyed her instincts as they pushed her to run faster.

To make Saint work harder to catch her.

Ahead of her, the trees thinned, and she spotted the raised L-shaped cabin. The moon cast silver light over it, making it as clear as day to her, and she set her sights on the steps that led up to the deck, determined to reach them before Saint reached her.

The cold snow numbed her feet and made it harder to run as she broke out into the clearing.

Saint didn't seem to have that problem.

She shrieked as he caught her from behind, twisted her and slammed her back into one of the thick posts that supported the front of the roof. A moan rolled up her throat as he claimed his prize, seizing her mouth in a hard, bruising kiss.

She wrestled her dress up, freeing her legs, and wrapped them around his waist and her arms around his neck as she kissed him. He groaned and pressed between her thighs, sending another thrill chasing through her as his body met hers and her thoughts spiralled, becoming a frantic blur of things she wanted to do to him, and things she wanted him to do to her.

Saint clutched her backside, ripping another moan from her, and pinned her to him, pressing the hardness in his jeans against her as he moved with her.

She groaned as he mounted the steps, as he kicked the door open and carried her inside. The heat of the fire washed over her, but it couldn't compete with the flames that licked through her veins as she kissed Saint, as he kicked the door closed behind them and walked with her.

Not towards the bedroom.

She broke the kiss, intending to guide him towards it, but could only groan as he laid her down in front of the stone fireplace, settling her on the thick fur. Her heart thundered as he released her and drew back, as he supported his weight on his left arm and gazed down at her, hunger darkening his eyes.

"Your shoulder." She lifted her hand and feathered her fingers over his right shoulder, careful not to apply any pressure in case she hurt him.

He didn't take his eyes off hers. "It's fine. Not sure I can feel pain when I'm with you. Can't feel anything but this... need."

She felt the same way. Her head was foggy with desire, her body trembling with an ache for him to caress it, and she felt sure she would go mad if he didn't kiss her again soon.

"I need you, Holly," he rumbled and his eyebrows pinched, his nostrils flaring as he looked her over, setting her on fire with the heat of his gaze. His eyes lifted back to lock with hers. "But we'll take things slow... Whatever you want to do is fine by me. I don't want to pressure—"

Holly seized his nape and pulled him down to her, kissed him hard to silence him because what she wanted was to satisfy this hunger he had ignited in her, to ease it before it drove her crazy. She didn't want slow. She didn't want to pace herself at all. She wanted him. All of him. Nothing held back.

And she wanted that forever.

Felt sure of it as she kissed him, as he settled his weight on her and kissed her back, his lips soft against hers as he slowed the kiss, apparently determined not to rush her. While she appreciated it in a way, she also wanted to scream.

She had waited too long for a male like Saint, had honestly believed she would never feel this, would never find him, and that she would spend the whole of her life alone.

Now everything she wanted was right here in her arms, within her reach.

And she was taking it.

Taking him.

She pressed her hand to his chest, careful to avoid his injury, and pushed, caught him off guard so he couldn't resist her. He grunted as he rolled, as she followed him and ended up on top of him, astride his hips.

She planted her hands to his chest as he stared up at her, shock rippling across his handsome face.

"I don't want to wait." She attacked the buttons of his shirt, almost growling when a few of them gave her trouble as her fingers shook, the thought of touching Saint making her a little giddy.

Saint relaxed into the fur, didn't fight her as she worked her way downwards, as she slowly parted his shirt with each button she undid. She stared at that V of muscles she exposed, growing hotter with every inch of him she revealed, and bit her lip and groaned when she finally undid the last button and his shirt fell open.

"Gods, you're glorious," she breathed.

Saint chuckled softly.

She turned it into a groan by planting her palms against the broad, hard slabs of his pectorals and stroking her fingers over them. The short dark hairs that covered them tickled her as she explored him, her pace more leisurely now that she had what she wanted.

Him—almost naked.

The sight of him was too good to rush though, and so was the way he reacted as she ventured lower, as she teased the ropes of his stomach and found a dark treasure trail she wanted to follow. He groaned and lifted his head off the furs, his brown eyes gaining a gold glow as they tracked her hands.

"Holly," he murmured.

She moaned at the way he said her name, so passion-drenched and filled with need. She liked it. Was sure she would never tire of hearing him say it in that way, as if she was killing him, as if he would go mad too if she didn't do something to give him relief soon.

Holly eased lower, moving to sit on his thighs.

Her hands met the waist of his jeans and she shivered as she brushed her palms along them, from his hips to just below his navel, and felt the hard outline of his erection. He groaned and tipped his hips up, pressing it into her hands. The calm that had come over her instantly dissipated and she ignored Saint's chuckle as she tore at his jeans, flooded with a hunger to see all of him.

She gripped the waist of his jeans and pulled them down, silencing him as she revealed him.

Oh gods.

He was big, beautifully hard, and just the sight of him had her wild with a need to feel him inside her. Saint stilled right down to his breathing as she lifted her right hand and she could feel the heat of his gaze as he watched her lowering it. Her breath trembled from her as she stared at his rigid length, trying not to overthink what she was doing, because she didn't want to be nervous.

She licked her lips, only realised what she had done when it tore a strained groan from Saint. Her heart leaped into her throat. She hadn't meant to insinuate that she wanted to lick him, hadn't really thought about it.

But now it was all she could think about.

She wanted to taste him.

She mustered her courage and dropped her fingers, shivered as she made contact with his rigid shaft.

Saint's head dropped, hitting the floorboards hard, and she flicked a glance at him, lingered as she found him lying with his head tipped back, his neck corded and every muscle of his torso tensed as she touched him. Gods. She stared at him, entranced by all his strength as she stroked her fingers down his cock. He groaned and tensed further, his shaft kicking against her fingers.

Rather than startled, she felt empowered.

How would he react if she kissed him?

Licked?

Heat scalded her cheeks. Sucked him?

She wanted to find out. Before she even knew what she was doing, she had leaned over him and was running her tongue up the length of him. Saint arched to meet her, his big body shuddering, making her feel even more powerful. She explored him with her tongue, from root to crown, and wrapped her lips around him. Groaned. He was hot in her mouth, but silky smooth against her tongue as she laved him.

When her tongue swept over the blunt head of him, she tasted him, a drop of seed on her tongue that had a startling effect on her.

She growled, a fierce need to make him give her more rushing through her, making her grip him with her hand and suck him harder. He grunted and his left hand lowered, tangled in her hair as she moved her mouth on him, hungry for another taste.

"Holly." Saint gripped her hair as that moan leaked from him, began moving her on him as he pumped his hips.

She growled and gripped them in both hands, pinned him and sucked him, forcing him to submit to her. The primal need to taste him grew stronger, had her snarling and resisting him as he tried to lift her head.

"Holly," Saint said, his tone commanding, but gentle. "Let me go and I'll give you what you need."

Oh gods.

She trembled at the thought, was quick to release him and lift her head. Her gaze collided with his and her brow furrowed when she saw in it that he meant those words, that he could ease this wild need building inside her, one she feared was going to take control again.

Saint dropped his hand to her jaw, smoothed his palm across it as he held her gaze. She eased back as he sat up, kept looking into his eyes, seeing a promise in them, one that had her trusting him because she knew deep in her heart that he would come good on it. He would tame this wild, primal, and frightening part of her.

She only had to submit to him.

She breathed through the urge to growl that came over her as she thought that, tamped down the need to seize command of things again, and managed to get herself under control.

Saint reached for the shoulders of her satin dress, sending a tremble through her as he made contact, his thumbs brushing her bare skin. The satin sliding over her skin made her shiver, made her nipples pucker as Saint's gaze fell to her breasts. She was hyper-aware of him as he leaned towards her, as he reached behind her to the zipper of her dress and lowered it, the sound loud in the thick air. A moan fell from her lips as he kissed her throat, licked close to her nape, and her eyes slipped shut as she leaned her head away from him, unable to resist the urge to give him better access to her neck.

His own moan joined hers as his bare chest brushed hers, as he finished lowering the zipper and eased back, taking hold of the shoulders of her dress again. It slipped down over her breasts, sending a thousand shivers cascading over her skin, and the heat of Saint's gaze seared her as his eyes dropped to her chest.

He pulled her up onto her knees as he dropped his head, and she arched backwards as his lips brushed her left nipple, agonising heat shimmering over her skin from that point. Her dress pooled around her spread thighs, teasing her oversensitive flesh as Saint pulled her nipple into his mouth and sucked it, rolled it between his teeth and had her pressing forwards, consumed by a need for more.

He gave it to her by lifting her dress, his hands burrowing beneath it to cup her backside. His fingers pressed into her flesh through her panties, parted her and dipped lower. She tensed and rose up on her knees, moaned as his fingers brushed between her plush petals.

"Gods," Saint muttered darkly, moved to her other breast and sucked on it, harder this time as his fingers delved between her thighs, as he stroked them over her flesh. He broke away from her and kissed up her chest, murmuring huskily, "You're so wet."

She was. Was that a bad thing? She hoped it wasn't, and then found she didn't care when Saint tore her panties away, when he cupped and stroked her, found her bundle of nerves and sent her shooting into the stratosphere.

Her cheeks burned as she rocked against his fingers, unable to stop her hips from moving, a slave to the need building inside her. Saint only made it worse as he trailed a finger upwards from her nub to her sheath and pressed inside a little.

She growled, couldn't hold it back as desire for something else filling her there flooded her. She didn't want his finger. She tried to wriggle free, managed to get her hand between them and find his shaft. She gripped and stroked it, fever burning her up as she thought about it inside her. When she tried to move to make it happen, Saint stopped her, his grip on her hip too strong for her to win against him.

"I want this to feel good," he husked against her throat, licked it and ripped a moan from her as his tongue flicked the lobe of her ear. "Need to get you ready. There's no rush. I'm not going anywhere."

Her primal instincts weren't listening to him, or to her, had her restless even when he pressed a finger inside her and they tried to hijack control again. Pleasure built inside her as he pumped her slowly. When he added another finger, stretching her, the tension inside her eased again, her instincts to mount him and take him falling away, replaced by a desperate need for more.

She moaned and kissed him, stroked his length as she thought about him inside her, as he filled her with his fingers.

She was close, balancing on the precipice, just needed another push.

She growled when Saint denied her, when he withdrew his fingers and removed her hand from him, but it faded into nothing as he pulled her dress up and discarded it. Calm washed through her as he fisted his cock, as he clutched her backside and lifted her. She shuffled towards him, her eyes on his length, aching with a need to have it inside her.

She gripped his left shoulder as he raised her higher, as he pressed his hand to the small of her back to draw her closer and reached around her thigh to hold himself again. She shivered, moaned and closed her eyes as he brushed the blunt head through her folds. As he nudged inside.

When he tried to take it slow, she growled again. She didn't want to draw this out. Her need of him was too painful, had her going out of her mind. She pressed back onto him, flinched a little as he stretched her and it stung, but the pleasure of him filling her was too intense for her to care. He groaned as she sank onto him, as she drew him into her heat. Her eyes opened, slowly widening as he claimed her backside and lifted her slightly before driving deeper into her.

Oh, she could get used to this.

He captured her mouth as he moved her on his cock, each delicious long stroke of it both satisfying her and maddening her. She rolled her hips, couldn't stop herself from participating, began riding him when he groaned, showing her that he liked it.

Holly shuffled her feet forwards, trying not to dislodge him as she wriggled onto them. He leaned over her slightly as she moved on him, kissed him and gripped his shoulder, riding him hard. He groaned and growled, gripped her hips and pumped her harder, faster, but it still wasn't enough. She wanted more. Needed more.

Sweat trickled down her spine, dampened her chest and made her stick to Saint as they moved together, their fast breaths mingling with each choppy kiss as they both reached for a release that wouldn't come.

Why wouldn't it come?

Her face screwed up, frustration rolling through her. That frustration only became fury as Saint pulled out of her, but it was gone in a heartbeat as he spun her away from him and brought her back down on his cock, spearing her from behind.

His breath fanned her nape as he clutched her thigh, holding her off him, and pumped her hard and fast, ripping a moan from her with each thrust. His other hand delved between her thighs and she cried out as he stroked and teased her, breathed harder as the need mounting inside her reached a crescendo but still refused to break.

Holly growled and reached over her head, clutched Saint's nape and pulled him to her, clawed at him and scented blood. He growled, sending a thrill rushing through her, and she clawed again, on fire with a need only one thing could sate.

"You sure?" he muttered and licked her neck, had shivers chasing over her as she ached for him to go through with it, to give her what she wanted.

"Yes," she cried as Saint drove into her, as he kissed her nape again.

"This is forever, Holly."

Was he determined to make her mad at him?

The sensible part of her said he was only trying to give her an out, but the rest of her said to hell with it. This was what she wanted. Saint. Forever.

"Forever with the man I love?" She panted those words. "Think I can handle that."

Saint stilled. Infuriating bear.

"Man you love?"

She growled and twisted, unable to wait another second. He fell forwards as she tried to move to face him, and she ended up on her back on the furs with him on top of her. He pressed his hand into the floor, holding himself off her, his dark eyes searching hers.

"You love me?" he whispered.

She nodded. "I love you."

He smiled, warming her to her bones. "I love you too."

But he still didn't look as if he was going to bite her.

She was about to take matters into her own hands when he reared back, flipped her onto her front and filled her again in one hard thrust. She swayed forwards, groaned as he grabbed her and pulled her up to him, sitting again.

Cried out as his fangs plunged into her nape.

Pleasure detonated inside her, rolled through every inch of her to stun her as he thrust deep inside her, his length throbbing as he spilled, as she quivered and milked him. Bliss ebbed and flowed through her as he gently moved inside her, as he held her with his fangs, and it wasn't only hers. It was his too. It curled through her together with his feelings, love that she could sense in him now.

When he finally released her and pulled out of her, she twisted to face him, settled herself astride his thighs and kissed him. The taste of her blood on his tongue ignited another fierce hunger, one she obeyed as she pushed up on her knees, as she caught his cheek and turned his head.

Sank her fangs into his nape.

He groaned and growled, and she moaned with him, the earthy taste of him on her tongue sending another fierce hit of pleasure rolling through her.

She forced herself to release him, eased back and stared into his eyes, catching the love shining in them as he gazed at her, as their bond slowly wove them together. Beautiful. Unbreakable.

"Love you," he murmured, brushed his knuckles across her cheek and looked at her in a way she thought a male never would.

As if she was his entire world.

"Love you too." She rewarded him with a kiss, one that warmed her all over and made her feel light inside.

She had come to Cougar Creek to escape being unable to find a male, and instead she had run into her mate.

A bear who had taken her captive, but in the end, she had been the one to steal something from him.

She had stolen his heart.

And now he was hers.

Forever.

The End

ABOUT THE AUTHOR

Felicity Heaton is a New York Times and USA Today best-selling author who writes passionate paranormal romance books. In her books she creates detailed worlds, twisting plots, mind-blowing action, intense emotion and heart-stopping romances with leading men that vary from dark deadly vampires to sexy shape-shifters and wicked werewolves, to sinful angels and hot demons!

If you're a fan of paranormal romance authors Lara Adrian, J R Ward, Sherrilyn Kenyon, Kresley Cole, Gena Showalter, Larissa Ione and Christine Feehan then you will enjoy her books too.

If you love your angels a little dark and wicked, her best-selling Her Angel romance series is for you. If you like strong, powerful, and dark vampires then try the Vampires Realm romance series or any of her stand alone vampire romance books. If you're looking for vampire romances that are sinful, passionate and erotic then try her London Vampires romance series. Or if you like hot-blooded alpha heroes who will let nothing stand in the way of them claiming their destined woman then try her Eternal Mates series. It's packed with sexy heroes in a world populated by elves, vampires, fae, demons, shifters, and more. If sexy Greek gods with incredible powers battling to save our world and their home in the Underworld are more your thing, then be sure to step into the world of Guardians of Hades.

If you have enjoyed this story, please take a moment to contact the author at **author@felicityheaton.com** or to post a review of the book online

Connect with Felicity:
Website – http://www.felicityheaton.com
Blog – http://www.felicityheaton.com/blog/
Twitter – http://twitter.com/felicityheaton
Facebook – http://www.facebook.com/felicityheaton
Goodreads – http://www.goodreads.com/felicityheaton
Mailing List – http://www.felicityheaton.com/newsletter.php

FIND OUT MORE ABOUT HER BOOKS AT:
http://www.felicityheaton.com